"I want you, Melinda."

"You'll get over it."

Her words might have been flippant, but every muscle in her body tensed as if for war.

"There's only one way I want to be over you. Naked. In a nice soft bed, with our clothes strewn across the floor."

"Wish all you want. It's not going to happen."

She tossed her hair over her shoulder and looked out the passenger window. Her body language couldn't be clearer. She was going to ignore him.

But he had no intention of letting her do so, not after he'd glimpsed the simmering heat in her eyes.

"I'm taking you to a houseboat on the St. John's River. It'll be private and romantic. The boat is fully stocked with food."

"I'm not hungry."

He lowered his voice. "You will be."

"Don't you get it? I don't want you."

"You will," he promised. "You will."

Dear Harlequin Intrigue Reader,

Need some great stocking stuffers this holiday season for yourself and your family and friends? Harlequin Intrigue has four dynamite suggestions—starting with three exciting conclusions.

This month, veteran romantic suspense author Rebecca York wraps up her special 43 LIGHT STREET trilogy MINE TO KEEP with *Lassiter's Law*, and Susan Kearney finishes her action-packed HIDE AND SEEK miniseries with *Lovers in Hiding*. Julie Miller, too, closes out the MONTANA CONFIDENTIAL quartet with her book *Secret Agent Heiress*. You won't want to miss any of these thrilling titles.

For some Christmastime entertainment, B.J. Daniels takes you west on a trip into madness and mayhem with a beautiful amnesiac and a secret father in her book *A Woman with a Mystery*.

So make your list and check out Harlequin Intrigue for the best gift around...happily ever after.

Happy holidays from all of us at Harlequin Intrigue.

Sincerely,

Denise O'Sullivan
Associate Senior Editor
Harlequin Intrigue

LOVERS IN HIDING
SUSAN KEARNEY

HARLEQUIN®

TORONTO • NEW YORK • LONDON
AMSTERDAM • PARIS • SYDNEY • HAMBURG
STOCKHOLM • ATHENS • TOKYO • MILAN • MADRID
PRAGUE • WARSAW • BUDAPEST • AUCKLAND

ISBN 0-373-22644-6

LOVERS IN HIDING

ABOUT THE AUTHOR

Susan Kearney used to set herself on fire four times a day; now she does something really hot—she writes romantic suspense. While she no longer performs her signature fire dive (she's taken up figure skating), she never runs out of ideas for characters and plots. A business graduate from the University of Michigan, Susan now writes full-time. She resides in a small town outside Tampa, Florida, with her husband and children and a spoiled Boston terrier.

Books by Susan Kearney

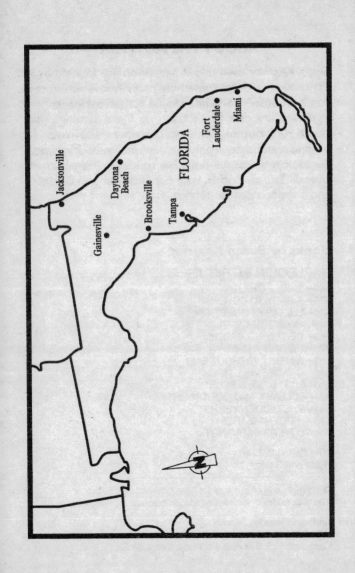

CAST OF CHARACTERS

Clay Rogan—Alias: Viper. Code breaker extraordinare, he's the CIA's top cryptanalyst. His job is to keep Melinda safe, but can he find the key to unlock her heart?

Melinda Murphy—One day she's living a normal life, the next day she's in extreme danger from a past she can't remember and a man she'll never forget.

Jake Cochran—The brother Melinda doesn't know.

Lionell Tower—The director of the CIA.

Sam Bronson—Is the message he left on Melinda's answering machine a key to solving the mystery of who is after her?

Herbert Silverberg—A man on a thirty-year mission.

Barry Lee—Nobel Prize-winning reporter. He's willing to risk his life to see justice done.

Aleksei Polozkova and Jon Khorkina—Agents for the CIA. But whose side are they on?

Prologue

Clay Rogan had never before been ordered into the director of operation's office of the CIA. Although he worked daily at the imposing building in McLean, Virginia, the prospect of meeting the director had him curious and edgy. The legendary director was responsible for all covert operations—far from Clay's normal turf in cryptanalysis.

After the D.O. had left an urgent message in the Hot Inbox file on Clay's computer, he'd hoped he wasn't about to be transferred to another division. Clay loved his work, took enjoyment in eighteen-hour days. He loved solving puzzles and breaking codes and, while his six-foot-six frame made him seem more suited for active pursuits, nothing provided him with as much pleasure as giving his brain a good workout. A ride on his motorcycle came in only a close second. Although Clay had trained at the renowned Farm in Camp Peary with other CIA recruits, he led a relatively normal life. He worked in an office, in front of a computer screen, scrutinizing bursts of satellite transmissions in an attempt to decode messages sent by foreign agents' transmitters.

As a master in his field, Clay had worked his way up from rookie and whiz kid to head of the crypt-analysis division. Early on, his superiors had recognized his linguistic abilities and intuitive knack for breaking code by spotting patterns where others could not. He'd earned the nickname Viper when he'd broken a Chinese code that had been composed of snakelike curves that had mystified other experts for years.

But to Clay, going into the field was as far-fetched an idea as dogs barking in Morse code. Sure, he'd taken the same basic courses required of all operatives—in detecting explosives, carrying out surveillance and countersurveillance operations, mastering a variety of weapons, and running counterintelligence, counternarcotics and paramilitary operations—but those activities were far outside his primary area of expertise.

So he had no idea why he'd been ordered to the D.O.'s office. Under normal circumstances he'd hesitate to venture onto the super-secret fifteenth floor, but the message in his Hot file this morning had left him no alternative.

He was to report to the D.O. himself. And tell no one.

Highly unusual. Highly irregular. Orders normally came down through channels.

The moment Clay arrived, the D.O.'s secretary ushered him into the opulent office. Although he'd never met the head of one of the most important departments in the government, he'd seen the director on television many times, reporting to Congress and briefing the Senate.

Up close, Lionel Tower's pit bull face looked even more tenacious than on the little screen. The man leaned aggressively forward, making Clay think his bark could be as bad as his bite. Yet, the moment Clay entered, the director graciously rose and came around his desk to shake hands, his spit-shined shoes squeaking.

"Thank you for coming so promptly."

Clay saw no reason to respond to the rhetorical comment. Both men knew he hadn't been given a choice. When the director commanded, his agents obeyed with an extra snap in their step. Obeyed not just because the director was in charge; the man was famous for turning more foreign spies into double agents than any other operative in the agency's long and convoluted history. He had earned their respect.

The hand that grasped Clay's had short, ragged nails, bit low on the fingertips. The palm was hard, cool and powerful. The director gestured for Clay to sit and then, surprisingly, pulled up a chair alongside him instead of returning behind his desk—a friendly action that made Clay even more wary.

"I'm sure you're curious about why you're here, so I'll get right to the point." Tower peered at Clay with a hopeful expression. "I'd like your help in a little matter."

Little? The D.O. didn't involve himself in little matters. He left that for underlings. But Clay kept his expression neutral. "Yes, sir?"

"Almost thirty years ago, a married couple worked for the agency. Both of them were operatives. The woman was killed and a short time later, her husband died in a mysterious car accident that we think was a hit. Their three children survived, and the agency hired a lawyer to find homes for the kids. Those children are now adults. I believe they're in danger."

"Sir?" Was the D.O. asking Clay to protect them? That was so far from his area of expertise, he had trouble believing that someone who had access to his file would have chosen him for the job.

"The name of the eldest, their only son, is Jake Cochran. Ever heard of him?"

"Should I have, sir?"

"Jake grew up in foster homes. When he graduated from high school, he tracked down the attorney we hired decades ago and tried to find his sisters."

"The kids were split up? I thought Family Services tries to keep them together."

"Together they would have been easier to track. Since we feared for their safety, it was decided the kids would be separated." Tower paused, no doubt regrouping his thoughts. "The parents were damn fine operatives, the best, so it's not surprising that Jake Cochran established one of the premier detective agencies in Florida. All the while, he kept searching for his sisters."

"Did he find them, sir?"

"He only just located them."

Clay frowned. "I don't understand, sir."

He didn't like the idea of children being separated. Families should stick together, and he sincerely hoped the D.O. didn't want him to have anything to do with keeping the siblings apart.

"Jake found adoption records with his sisters' new names and addresses. He mailed them each a letter with old photographs and copies of his mother's papers. He also hired bodyguards to protect both his sisters.''

Clay put the pieces together quickly. ''The siblings are in danger because of the mother's documents?''

''You catch on fast. Jake and one sister have already gone underground. I want you to befriend the third sister, get her to trust you.''

''Am I permitted to know why?''

Tower chuckled. ''Absolutely. I need you to decode the documents.''

Clay finally understood why he'd been chosen for this mission. He currently worked with the newest state-of-the-art codes, but his hobby was deciphering old codes like the one the special agent might have used almost thirty years ago. Information on his hobby was most assuredly right in his file along with his favorite flavor of chewing gum, cherry; his preferences in women, model-thin blondes with small, high breasts and cool intelligence; and his favorite leather jacket size—extra large.

Still he was reluctant to take on the full assignment. Although he itched to try his luck with the old codes, protection wasn't his specialty and he didn't want to get someone killed. ''Sir, surely there are people much more qualified than me to protect the sister—''

''Melinda Murphy.''

''To protect Ms. Murphy—''

''You're the best qualified cryptanalyst for the job.'' The D.O. gave him a significant look. Clay didn't have to know the man well to understand that he was expected to keep his mouth shut and commit the instructions for this assignment to memory. But why hadn't the D.O. assigned another, more qualified agent to protect the woman and allowed Clay to do what he did best—decode? Was he missing something? Or was Clay just annoyed because he didn't yet have all the puzzle's pieces to analyze? After a taut silence, the D.O. finally added, "We don't want to alert anyone else to the situation."

We? So now it was a team effort. But it would be Clay's ass on the line, and the girl's too if he screwed up. "May I ask why *we* are keeping this operation to just us, sir?"

His expertise wouldn't come into play until later, after he'd gained the woman's trust, and Clay hoped he wouldn't be asked to betray her to bring the code to the agency. Despite his credentials as a fully trained covert operative, he didn't like lies.

"Because I suspect someone inside the CIA is running his own secret operation against these siblings."

Clay swallowed hard, suddenly understanding the covert nature of this extremely dangerous assignment. No wonder the D.O. wanted him to work alone—less chance of a leak. And a leak could be critical since his job was to ferret out a traitor within the CIA.

"Do I—"

"No backup. No partners. Just you with a direct phone line to me."

"And my current assignments?"

"I'll handle those. Viper, you take care of the woman. Melinda Murphy lives in Daytona Beach, Florida." The director handed him a file. "Just find her, decode the papers and bring the results back to me. Only to me."

Chapter One

Time to play.

Melinda Murphy loaded her long board and new Aerotech sail and mast onto her car's rack and headed for Ponce Inlet, a peninsula just south of Daytona Beach that permitted cars on the beach. Once she parked on Florida's fabulous white sand, she wouldn't have far to carry her gear to the surf.

She sniffed the tangy salt air and appreciated the May sunshine as the wind whipped her hair through her open car window. She might just sail in her shorty, a wet suit that left her arms and legs bare to the water, since the air was warm enough to keep her comfortable. Although she knew the water temperatures would still be cool this time of year, she longed for the wetness against her skin. Besides, she'd warm up quickly as she beat into the wind, sailing through the large rolling waves that swelled, then gathered force as they crested and crashed onto the beach.

Even allowing time to drive back for a shower and a change of clothes, Melinda figured she had several good hours of sailing time. She had four hours until her next appointment, with a demanding lady, but one who'd recommended her to some very influential potential clients. Clients who could afford to pay a hundred bucks for a two-hour massage. Clients who had stressful jobs. Clients who would be happy to shell out more cash for additional pampering when Melinda opened her full-service salon, which would include facials and manicures, in the fall.

Melinda almost had enough money saved. The financing had been arranged to allow her to make a down payment and renovate the cute little house with a prime commercial location that she wanted to buy. Soon, all she'd worked and planned for would become reality, and she'd have the stability of her own business.

But for the next few hours, Melinda intended to put work out of her mind and enjoy the sunshine kissing her skin, the breeze dancing in her hair, the hot sand slipping between her toes. The beach wouldn't be crowded on a Thursday afternoon. She wouldn't have to watch out for the surfers catching their next wave or kids swimming or body surfing or tossing Frisbees.

She expected only dolphins, sand crabs and seagulls for company. Sure enough, as she turned onto the beach, it was relatively empty. A lone fisherman cast his line at the end of the pier. Several boats headed into the harbor around the point, and a seaplane flew northward up the coast.

Melinda sighed happily in expectation, turning her face up to the sun shining through her windshield, looking forward to a strenuous afternoon. A cottony cumulus cloud scudded over the sun, casting long shadows across the beach, and the shimmering waters darkened to a menacing gray. For a moment, Melinda shivered, memories of the disturbing package she'd received yesterday morning swimming through her thoughts like a shark circling prey.

She'd always known she had been adopted. But she'd been too busy struggling to survive to give her past much thought. After her adopted parents' divorce, there'd been barely enough money to put food on the table, never mind send her to college. So she'd earned her massage therapy license at age eighteen and had been responsible for her own bills ever since. Now, at twenty-five, she rarely thought of the past, and focused only on her future and the business she would soon open.

But the package she'd received yesterday from her biological brother had changed her world and her place in it. Melinda had a brother and a sister. Two siblings. She didn't find the facts particularly comforting. Large families meant more mouths to feed. More fights. More responsibilities.

As she turned her attention back to the present, she noticed a shiny blue sedan with two men in business suits following her vehicle down the beach. Wanting her privacy, she kept going, hoping they'd park far enough away that she wouldn't have to hear their conversation. She'd come to relax.

But the old letters, diaries and pictures that once belonged to her biological mother kept worming their way into her mind. Would her brother, Jake Cochran, come calling soon? What did he want from her?

And what about the sister, older by two years, that she'd never met? Would they look alike? Would her sister have Melinda's olive skin, tawny eyes and black hair? Her brother's letter had told her almost nothing about himself, but after she'd read his note, she'd picked up the phone and called him.

Jake hadn't answered, and she hadn't left a message on his voice mail, although she wasn't sure why. She'd told herself that with her hectic schedule, he wouldn't be likely to catch her in. And if he'd called back during an appointment with a client, she couldn't speak for long on her cell phone. It would simply be more convenient for her to call him back again later.

A glance in her rearview mirror revealed that the two men in the blue sedan hadn't yet parked, but were still trailing her down the beach. While the traffic was often bumper to bumper, there was lots of room now, and she felt a minor edge of alarm when their car followed hers so closely.

They had the entire beach to themselves. Why tailgate?

When they honked at her, she kept driving along the beach, obeying the ten-mile-per-hour speed limit, and ignored the men, hoping they just wanted to pick up a beach babe and would go away if she paid them no attention. Before, she'd welcomed the isolation. Now, she wished for the weekend crowd. But besides the fisherman who stood on the pier with his back to her, the only other person on the beach appeared to be a man on a motorcycle, maybe a half mile back, his silhouette black and razor sharp against the blowing sand.

At least she hadn't stopped and turned off her engine. She could simply keep driving, circle to the main road and report the creeps to the cops. She might lose a half hour of sailing time, but she knew trouble when she saw it.

However, when she tried to head back toward the road, the sedan blocked her. Quickly, more annoyed than frightened, she whipped the steering wheel the other way and made a skidding U-turn, her wheels sinking into wet sand and lapping waves. She easily made the turn and glanced over her shoulder, figuring she'd lost the men in suits.

Then she again spied the blue sedan on her tail, speeding toward her. It looked ready to ram her, smash her to a bloody pulp. She slammed her foot on the gas pedal.

Her car skidded like oil on a hot skillet. Failed to accelerate quickly enough.

The sedan rocketed into her car's trunk. Her car veered into the ocean and water rolled up to her tires, up to her bumper, onto the floorboards.

Soon it would be up to her neck, making her keep her head above water to avoid drowning. A huge wave lumbered over the hood like a runaway mule, kicked into her windows, tossed the car up and smashed it into another taller wall of dark water. She banged her head and fireworks shot off in a sea of darkness. Her airbag inflated.

And then her world turned black.

CLAY GUNNED HIS Harley down the beach, blasting a spray of sand behind him, skidding to a stop short of where Melinda Murphy's car had just been forced into the water by the blue sedan. At the first sign of trouble, he'd kicked his bike into gear, wishing he'd had more power. She wasn't going to die on his watch.

Running toward her, he flung his jacket behind him, stopping for only a few seconds to kick off his boots. His heart was hammering so hard he barely heard the roar of the waves pounding the rocks by the pier like a hammer. Barely noticed the cold water that numbed his extremities. Barely noticed how suddenly the sunshine was disappearing as thunderclouds thronged dark and dangerous overhead.

He refused to lose her. Not after he'd stayed awake, driving all night to reach her.

Yesterday, after learning he couldn't catch a commercial flight to Daytona's tiny airport, he'd chosen to ride his bike from Virginia to Florida. Maybe he should have chartered a special flight. Or flown into Orlando or Jacksonville. Or hired protection for her until he'd arrived to take over himself.

Wishing he could sprout fins, his frantic dash into the water slowed as he was forced to wade through the waist-high waves. He forged right by the blue sedan that had been caught by a wave and spun upside down, trapping its occupants inside.

Clay's clothes absorbed water, slowing his progress, but he lunged forward, straining every iota of energy out of his powerful thighs, breathing hard, balancing on each crest of water, praying he could make it to Melinda before she drowned.

His first assignment. He wouldn't blow it before it began. He wouldn't have a woman's life weighing on his conscience, wouldn't live with failure.

Fifteen minutes ago, at noon, when he'd reached Melinda's rented house, he hadn't been too alarmed that she wasn't there, especially after a neighbor told him that she'd driven off with her windsailer strapped to her car's rack. Clay had followed the helpful neighbor's directions to the beach, and he'd obeyed the speed limit. Now he wished he hadn't.

The tide was kidnapping her, holding her hostage in its fierce grip, the car bobbing and spinning and rolling like a sinking boat. The blue sedan fared no better. When the sand dropped from beneath his feet and the water reached his chest, he started swimming, his arms windmilling, his legs kicking.

Water was filling the inside of her car, each incoming wave pouring in with fierce surges. Fear of watching her sink before his eyes made his tired limbs fight through the water. If she disappeared completely before he reached her, he might not even find the vehicle. Right now he could only see her sailboard strapped to the roof, about to be washed under the surging water.

The blue sedan stayed afloat better than Melinda Murphy's car, and its occupants were trying to climb out onto the roof of their vehicle.

Clay cursed the powerful waves and the fate that had led him here. Doing too little. Too late.

His body wasn't made for swimming. He didn't have the lean lines of a swimmer. Built like a wrestler with too many heavy muscles that didn't want to float, he struggled, took in a mouthful of water. He choked, but kept going.

He had to reach her. Minutes counted. Seconds counted.

Finally he stroked alongside her car. Stretching his hand through the open window, he yanked open the door, reached inside and grabbed her. She wouldn't come free.

Damn it.

She must be wearing a seat belt.

Taking a quick breath, he prepared to dive under, but a surging wave lifted the car, for a few moments helping instead of hampering his rescue efforts. He reached past the airbag, unsnapped her seat belt and pulled her into his arms.

She didn't fight him. Didn't move. Remained completely limp.

Please don't be dead.

Eyes closed, unmoving, she floated in his arms like a mermaid that the sea had given up to him. Her color was pale, almost gray as death, but he didn't have time for CPR or mouth-to-mouth. Even the Heimlich maneuver was impossible in the high surf. First, he had to swim her to shore.

Although she didn't weigh much, the waves caught at her body, trying to tug her from him. Yet this time the wind and the rolling surges pushed them in the direction in which he wanted to go.

His lungs burned with effort as he struggled to carry her. Ignoring the pain in his chest and the cramps in his straining legs, he battled the surging waves, unable to use his hands to swim while he held her, trying to keep her head above water. He fought his way back and finally his feet touched sand. But he didn't have time to feel relief.

Didn't have time to consider how long it would take the men in the blue sedan to give up their fragile perch on the car's roof and make a swim for the beach. Didn't have time to consider how long it would take them to be within shooting range.

On the beach, he collapsed to his knees beside Melinda and leaned over to examine her. He had no idea whether she had a pulse, doubted he could find it with his wet and cold fingers. One quick glance at her gray skin told him she wasn't breathing. How long had it been? Two minutes? Three? Four and she'd suffer brain damage.

Brain damage. The ugly words cut like a razor, sharp and painful. Tilting her head back, he cleared an airway, pinched her nostrils shut. Then he placed his mouth over hers and breathed.

"Come on, Melinda." He spoke to her, each time blowing more air into her mouth.

"Breathe."

"Breathe."

Out of his peripheral vision, he saw the men in suits start their swim to shore, like sharks scenting prey. They'd drifted way out, giving him extra minutes to ensure her safety, which would do him no good if she didn't regain consciousness.

"Damn it. I told you to breathe."

Her eyelids fluttered. Maybe she responded to the urgency in his tone. Maybe her lungs needed time to fill with air, but whatever the reason, he couldn't have been more relieved when she coughed. He turned her head to help her to spit out water. Even a teaspoonful in the lungs was enough to drown a person.

Her trembling hand rose to her head and she mumbled, "Hurts."

Her eyes opened, and her pupils were very large,

surrounded by the creamiest hue of caramel he'd ever seen. Dark hair covered her forehead, and when he smoothed back the wet strands, he discovered a lump the size of a golf ball there. Just looking at the knot starting to discolor made him wince. She needed ice to keep the swelling down. Unfortunately, he had none.

He held up two fingers. "How many?"

"Four?"

"Great, you're seeing double."

"That's why there's two of you," she muttered then closed her eyes.

"Oh no you don't. Melinda, you can't go to sleep. You have a head injury. Maybe a concussion."

"Hurts."

Helpless, she lay in his arms, but at least her deadly gray pallor had been replaced by a much more healthy-looking olive tone. "You need a doctor."

"I need—" Her eyes suddenly opened again, and she bolted into a sitting position, wincing at the pain the effort cost her. "Who are you?"

She sounded as suspicious as an operative on his first assignment, and he almost smiled. He supposed many women might be frightened by his appearance, black leather pants and a black T-shirt—all sopping wet. His size alone could intimidate most men, and he hadn't bothered shaving this morning, so his jaw sported more than a five-o'clock shadow. For her to wake up in the arms of a stranger had to be unnerving, especially one as scruffy-looking as he probably was.

Of course, she wasn't exactly ready for a beauty pageant either—not with that bump on her head that was starting to turn a wicked shade of purple. But with her tight tank top plastered to her breasts and short shorts that outlined her hips, she appeared to be a prime candidate for a wet T-shirt competition.

Thank God, a man like him would never be attracted to his charge. He didn't go for petite, curvy brunettes with eyes like melted taffy. He preferred his women cool, blond and intellectual. Melinda Murphy, with her delicate jaw and suspicious glare looked precisely like the type of woman who was trouble with a capital T.

She'd nearly died, he reminded himself, and she wasn't out of danger yet. Luckily the escalating wind and rising current were on their side, hindering her pursuers' progress back to shore. Within moments, they would be swept around the point.

He didn't want to scare her by mentioning the men after her, not while her hands trembled and her eyes reflected confusion. "I'm Clay Rogan." He pointed to the choppy sea, noting that the blue sedan and the swimming men were now totally out of view and around the bend. "When I saw your car go under—"

Bewilderment filled her eyes, and she frowned, her full lips forming a lusty pout full of suspicion. "My car? Underwater?"

"I'm lucky I got you out. I'm afraid I couldn't do much about the—"

Her head jerked back and forth in denial, her eyes wildly searched the churning waves as if she'd lost a dear friend. "I don't suppose you nabbed my purse?"

"Sorry."

Her bottom lip quivered. Oh, hell, she was going to cry.

"Don't cry."

He hated when women cried, because then he gave in to their demands and hated himself for it later. Only, this half-drowned mermaid wasn't making demands. Yet she was so suspicious of him that he didn't know whether to feel sorry for her.

Her eyes brimmed.

"Don't," he repeated softly but firmly, as he would to an injured child.

She paid absolutely no attention to his demand. Tears overflowed her eyes and rolled down her cheeks.

He bit back a curse and gently lifted her into his lap, cradling her against his chest, tucking her head beneath his chin. Her entire body shook, a sob escaped and instead of offering her additional reassurances, his first thought was how holding her in his arms made him feel like keeping her there for a long time. She had a toned body, teasing curves and a bottom lip he wanted to taste.

What the hell was wrong with him? The woman was crying and all he could think about was her bottom lip? Forcing his thoughts back to practical matters wasn't easy, although usually his focused mind stayed on the subjects he intended it to. But her combination of strength and defenselessness called to him on a level he couldn't quite comprehend. He only knew he had to regain control of himself, before he did something stupid—like kiss her.

"Are you in pain? You need a doctor?"

"Not a doctor. I need a psychiatrist."

A shrink? Was she crazy?

Actually he must be the insane one around here. She wanted a shrink. And he wanted to kiss her. What kind of a secret agent was he anyway?

A bad one.

Damn it! This mission would be hard enough with a reasonably sane woman. And Melinda Murphy seemed anything but reasonable. Or sane. In fact, she hadn't made much sense since the moment she'd opened those soulful toffee-colored eyes and raised his protective armor.

Perhaps he needed to humor her. "Okay. Why do you need a psychiatrist?"

"Because I have no memory."

"What do you mean you have no memory?"

"Which word don't you understand?" she countered. But the tears still rolling over her cheeks took the sting out of her strong words.

He suspected she was trying to be brave, especially since he could feel her trembling. So he gentled his tone even more. "You don't remember your accident?"

She shook her head and angrily wiped away her tears with the back of her hand. "Tell me what happened. Maybe it'll come back to me."

Finally, a good suggestion. But they needed to get out of here in case anyone else showed up. Before the men he'd seen swimming around the point made it to shore and headed back here for Melinda.

Still, Clay hesitated, knowing she was in a fragile emotional state. He couldn't be so callous, wasn't so pressed for time that he couldn't make a few explanations.

Clay ignored the storm clouds darkening overhead. They were already soaked, their clothing sticking to them like a swimsuit. A little rain would only wash off the salt. "When I arrived on the beach, I saw a blue sedan force your car into the water."

She straightened in his lap, pulling her head from under his chin. She looked up and down the beach, her spine stiff, her arms crossed over her chest defensively. "I don't see another car."

"The vehicle chased you into the ocean. And sank."

"Really?"

She didn't believe him. He could see it in her eyes, which glinted like ice glimmering through a fog, and in the stiff way she scooted off his lap and stood, looking uncertainly around her. But he could no longer point out the two swimming men, since they'd made it around the point. Or the tire tracks that the waves had washed away.

She spied his black leather jacket, his boots, then his motorcycle, and took several steps back, her eyes narrowed with the wariness of a cornered cat.

"You don't remember the accident at all?"

"Must be the bump on my head."

"Okay, let's backtrack. Did you notice the blue sedan following you from your house?"

"I don't remember." Her bottom lip, slightly purple with cold, quivered again, but she fought back the tears with a valiant sigh.

"Hey, don't let it upset you. You obviously got whacked upside the head. Maybe that made you forget. But even if the head injury didn't cause your memory loss, unless they're trained to notice, most citizens won't pick up a tail.''

The information didn't seem to reassure her. If anything, his words made her even more vigilant as she curled her fingers into fists. She shivered and looked at him as if he were a crab that had crawled out from beneath a rock.

''Citizen? What are you, some kind of military—''

''I work in an office on a computer,'' he told her. If there was one thing Clay hated, it was lies. Yet the truth would frighten her and make her trust him less than she already did.

''Then how do you know about tails?''

He shrugged, slipped on his boots, picked up his jacket and walked toward her, holding the jacket extended as a peace offering, intending to wrap her in its dry warmth. ''I watch TV like everybody else.''

Teeth chattering, she backed up, staying out of reach, even though she obviously needed his jacket. Her lips were definitely bluish purple and goose bumps rose on her flesh. ''How do I know *you* weren't the one who forced my car into the water?''

''On a motorcycle?''

Car tires had left imprints all over the beach but there was no way to prove which tracks belonged to which vehicles. Waves had washed away the critical ones that led directly to the water. ''You'll have to take my word, Melinda.''

As he said her name, she retreated again, her teeth chattering. ''Just how do you know my name?''

Damn! He didn't want to lie to her. It went against the grain. But if he told her he'd been sent by the CIA's director of operations to protect her, he'd be breaking his orders not to reveal his cover. Yet he needed her to trust him. Enough to let him look at the documents her brother had sent her.

"You told me your name when I pulled you out of the car."

"Liar!" She took another step back, spun on her heel and raced away from him as if her life depended on eluding him.

She'd called him a liar, and his jaw dropped in astonishment. How had she known he'd lied? She hadn't been conscious and couldn't know she hadn't mumbled to him. Why was she looking at him as if he were a criminal with violence on his mind?

He let her run, knowing he could easily catch her on his bike. But then he realized chasing her down with his Harley would frighten her even more.

And while he stood there second-guessing himself, the woman had a damn good head start. With a muffled oath, he took off after her, wondering how one small brunette could cause so much trouble. He should have ridden the Harley. Maybe if he scared her enough, she'd be more cooperative.

He wasn't cut out for this kind of work. As he pounded down the beach in his leather boots that weren't made for running any more than they were made for swimming, he thought once again that the director had made a mistake in choosing him for this assignment. He simply didn't have the experience to provide good protection. Didn't have the kind of practice necessary to handle Ms. Melinda Murphy.

With her tears and her sobs and her angry defiance, she'd twisted him around inside. She was manipulating him in a way he found impossible to fight.

Because she didn't fight fair. She used those feminine weapons that did a man in every time. But he couldn't let her big tawny eyes stop him from doing his job.

She ran like the gusting wind and straight into the thundering storm, her lean legs eating up the distance with remarkable speed. It took longer than he'd have guessed to catch her. Then, after he'd almost caught up, she put on a burst of speed and dashed straight toward the water.

"Oh no you don't."

He'd had enough swimming thank you very much. Lunging, he tackled her and they both fell, rolling in the sand. He landed on his back with her on his chest, snuggled between his thighs. For a moment those soft curves pressed to his body kindled a primitive response.

And then her knee lifted, aiming for his groin.

"Lady, I swear if you kick me in the balls, I'll deck you," he threatened, knowing he wouldn't and hoping she wouldn't realize it. Due to an oversize workload, Clay had gotten less than ten hours of sleep in the last five nights. Twenty-three-hour days of nonstop pressure were starting to catch up with him, fraying his temper, increasing his irritability. This assignment had pulled him off an important job—one that could make a difference in setting U.S. diplomatic policy for a decade. His reactions and temper reflected a measure of his frustration. He twisted to the side, rolling them until he ended up on top, with her on her back beneath him, her black hair splayed across the sand like an exotic fan.

Before she could scratch the flesh off his face, kick

him in the groin or chin, he pinned her wrists. She shook a stray lock of hair out of her way, her eyes burning coals of outrage. "Let me go, you biker bully."

"I won't hurt you."

She rolled her eyes at the raining sky. "Oh, sure. Like I'm really going to believe you."

Thunder roared overhead, pounding over them in flashing echoes. He paid no attention, focusing on the storm brewing beneath him. "Why shouldn't you believe me? I saved your life, lady."

"So you say."

"You should be grateful."

"Oh, thank you so much," she said with saccharine sweetness and mockery. "Now that I've thanked you, you'll let me go, right?"

He ignored her question. "Why did you run from me?"

She heaved a sigh of frustration and tried to shift him off by bucking her hips. He let her struggle, knowing she'd soon come to the conclusion that he was bigger and stronger, and she wasn't escaping until he got his answer and freed her of his own accord.

"Look, mister biker-dude."

"Don't call me that."

She arched a haughty eyebrow. "You haven't told me your name."

"I believe I did. It's Clay. Clay Rogan."

"Fine, Mr. Clay Rogan. I don't know you. I have no memory of you before opening my eyes on this beach to find you standing over me. You say someone else forced my car into the water. But my car isn't here. You say another car forced mine into the water, and guess what? That car isn't here either. Then you said I told you my name—an outright lie. Don't deny it, mister—you did lie."

"Okay, I admit that was a mistake. If I told you the truth, you wouldn't believe me."

"Why should I?"

"Exactly my point. Why bother with a difficult truth when you obviously didn't believe the easy stuff?" He paused to rein in his aggravation. "I assume, until you drove the car into the water, you had no idea you've been in danger?"

Her eyes widened, she struggled to free her wrists. He held her tighter.

She winced. "You said you wouldn't hurt me."

He loosened his grip slightly. "Will you get it through your stubborn head that the danger isn't from me. Someone is after you."

"So *you* say."

"Look, this all started before I got here. You do remember leaving your house and driving to the beach?"

"Mister. Clay," she amended, "you listen about as well as I remember."

What had he missed? As he searched her eyes, he saw a turbulence of emotions, fear, anger and hesitation. "Tell me again."

"I knew you'd lied about how you knew my name because I couldn't have possibly given you that information."

"Why not?"

All her sarcasm and sass evaporated, just as the rain poured down, soaking his back with slashing droplets of ice. "Because I haven't just forgotten the accident. I don't remember *anything*."

"Nothing?"

"Not my name. Not my address. Not even what I do for a living."

Chapter Two

She'd known the moment she opened her eyes on the beach that something was very, very wrong. Her heart pounded too hard, and her adrenaline had been sapped, her energy stolen as if she'd just run a marathon. Fear coiled through her body, leaving a sour taste in her mouth and twisting her gut into a hard knot, but she had no idea why she was so afraid.

She'd discerned her memory loss almost right away, and the realization knocked her for one doozy of a loop. While she gasped for air, her brain sucked in details of her surroundings; a wide beach pounded by rain and a devastatingly handsome, dangerous-looking man hovering over her, his grim expression as dark as the black leather clinging to his massive thighs.

Faced with the immediate threat of him, her memory loss shifted to a back burner. His eyes, green as the stormy sea and hard as the stone jetty, clued her in that he wasn't the brotherly or husbandly type. While she might know him, she had the distinct impression from his sharp curiosity that they were complete strangers. She didn't know his name, didn't rec-

ognize his stony face, and was positive that if she'd
met him before, she would remember something
about him. He carried the distinctive scent of masculine leather on his skin. When he spoke, his breath
carried an unusual cherry flavor that contrasted with
his tough-guy image. His wide-set, sea-green eyes
revealed anger and guilt, but she also glimpsed an
inkling of concern that reached beyond her fear. His
strong jaw, stubbled like a pirate's, and his generous
mouth, set with an arrogant firmness, suggested that
this man was accustomed to others obeying his com-
mands.

Not today she wouldn't. She didn't care if he had
shoulders wider than the Gulf Stream or more muscles than Hulk Hogan, he'd fed her an inedible story
that even a ten-year-old kid wouldn't swallow.

The fact that she currently couldn't remember her
age, her address or her name didn't mean she didn't
have a working brain. But it sure as hell was one
gargantuan handicap. If she had to lose her memory,
why couldn't it have happened among friends? Or
family? If she'd hit her head in a car accident—and
the knot on her head and the aches in her muscles
certainly felt as if she had—why couldn't she have
been rescued by the police, driven by paramedics to
a hospital?

Instead she'd lost her memory and ended up with
a menacing-looking hunk in black leather. She gazed
at the muscular arms holding her down, finding it
curious that he didn't sport tattoos. He wore no ear-
rings to accessorize, either. Maybe the man wasn't
as wild as he'd first appeared. He certainly didn't

seem to want to hurt her. He'd had ample opportunity, yet remained gentle.

He'd tackled her and landed so he'd taken the brunt of the fall. Even now, with her pinned beneath him, he spared her the crushing force of his full weight, while protecting her face from the teeming rain as he leaned over her and surveyed her with assessing eyes. Those eyes again. Caring eyes. Intelligent eyes.

He eased up on her wrists slightly. "When's your birthday?"

"I don't know."

"How old are you?"

"I don't know."

"Parlez-vous français?"

God! A multilingual biker. Did he have to sound so sexy when he spoke to her? "I don't speak French."

"But you understood the question."

"Don't you know phrases in languages you don't speak?" she countered, wondering how long this inquisition would go on, wondering what he intended to do with her when it was over. At the realization of his power over her and her helplessness to fight him, she shivered. He could take whatever he wanted from her, and this man seemed accustomed to taking.

Panic rose up her throat, and she reminded herself that he likely wouldn't have told her his name if he intended to hurt her.

As if reading her racing fears, Clay let out a frustrated sigh. "This is one hell of a mess. Let's hope your memory comes back real soon. Meanwhile, I'll have to hide you."

"Hide me?" She didn't like the sound of that at all. She didn't want to go anywhere with this man. She didn't know him. She didn't know herself enough to trust her judgment or believe the clear ring of tension in his voice.

"I need to keep you safe."

"Then take me to the cops," she suggested.

"You'll be safer with me than the cops." He rolled off her and tugged her to her feet, never releasing her wrist. "Come on. I'll explain on the way back to my bike."

The moment he released her, the ripping rain and slicing wind bombarded her like hail. She refused to miss the warmth of his arms. Instead, she told herself, she was glad he no longer pressed her back into the cold, wet sand. She didn't want to go anywhere with Clay Rogan—especially to his bike where he could spirit her away to some isolated place where she'd never be seen again.

Why couldn't she recall her family? Friends? Or maybe a wonderful husband who might be frantically searching for her even now? It finally occurred to her that if Melinda was her real name, as he claimed, then Clay could tell her more about herself.

"What's my last name?" she asked as he tugged her along the beach where the waves rolled in, attacked the sand, then receded in a white froth of sucking sounds.

"Murphy." The name evoked no emotions. Not even a sliver of recognition.

"Am I a student?"

"You're a massage therapist." She had no emotional reaction to that information either, but a fleeting tingle raced across her hands as if she could recall her fingers kneading muscles. Was the image a memory? Or something she'd envisioned when he mentioned her occupation? If he'd told her she was a teacher or a doctor, would she have had the same reaction and imagined chalk dust on her skin or a scalpel in her hands?

"Am I married?"

"No."

She couldn't decide whether his answer pleased her or not. While she could imagine how awful it would be to return to a loving husband or child and not recognize them, the idea of leaning on someone who loved her had its own merits.

The fact that Clay knew more about her than she knew about herself left an eerie hollowness in her that she wanted to fill with more facts. He could be making up the information, lying to her, and she'd never know, but why would he do that?

"Do I have family?"

"You were adopted, and your adoptive parents divorced when you were little."

Lightning flashed, zigzagging over the water and brightening the sky in a blaze of white light followed by cold, damp darkness. They needed to get off the beach, but her thoughts distracted her. In her mind, she saw a woman's face, just for a moment, and then it was gone. The woman was weeping, fat lonely tears. Another memory? Or her mind playing more tricks on her? Seconds later, thunder rolled across the beach with the razor-sharp wind, slicing the sand against them.

Clay pulled her into a run. "I'll tell you everything

once we get out of this weather. The most important thing you need to know is that I'm CIA and I was sent to protect you.''

Yeah, right. And she was Lois Lane. She dug her heels into the sand and tried to jerk him back. Only her action didn't go quite the way she planned. Clay simply had too much bulk for her to yank him to a halt. He kept going, as if her resistance was futile. However, while he failed to stop, she ended up flying forward, smacking into him with a force that made her knees wobble. To steady her, he let go of her wrist, and his arms came around her, anchoring her.

"If you wanted me to carry you, you could have just said so," he teased without the slightest smile, but the warmth in his tone calmed her a little.

She refused to lean into that warmth. "I suppose you can prove you're with the CIA."

He reached into his back pocket and took out very official-looking identification with his picture sealed beneath the plastic. In the picture his black hair was shorter, his jaw clean-shaven, but it was definitely him. But then, anyone could create fake documents with a computer and a good color printer.

"How come you didn't identify yourself earlier?" she asked without bothering to hide her doubts.

"I'm not supposed to." He frowned, as if breaking the rules was something he didn't do lightly. "But with your amnesia, it now seems necessary."

She glanced from the ID back to him, wishing she had her memory, wondering if she could be in some kind of trouble. Or maybe she was wrong. Despite how scared she'd felt earlier, she had no facts or memories to back up her conviction that she'd been fighting for her life. But whom had she been fighting? And why?

What could a massage therapist know that would be critical to her government? Had she had some important client who yakked in her ear while she rubbed the stress out of his shoulders?

And didn't the FBI handle domestic problems and the CIA operate overseas? What would the CIA want with *her,* a massage therapist? She tapped his ID. "You have an office I can call to verify this?"

"I'm undercover. I'm only allowed to check in after the first part of my mission is accomplished."

"How convenient."

His eyes narrowed as he accepted her insult and tossed her words back in her face. "It's not convenient at all. I'd prefer to have backup."

"Then why don't you have help?" she asked, wondering if she'd feel better or worse if he had an accomplice. An accomplice could verify his lie as well as the truth and then she'd have to outwit two of them to escape—not that she was doing so jam-up terrific with just him.

His lips moved but thunder roared so loudly, she couldn't hear his answer. When he dragged her against him, she instinctively yanked back. Found herself caught like a mosquito in a giant spiderweb.

Her stomach knotted so tightly, she had to fight to suck in air. He'd finally stopped trying to talk to her. She braced for a fist to her jaw or a jab to her churning stomach.

But he didn't so much as slap her.

Instead, inexorably, his superior strength overwhelmed her struggles and forced her chest right up against his, her hips cradled to the hard quadriceps in his thighs. Even with wet clothing between them, she could feel heat radiating from him, feel the frustration he'd kept locked beneath rigid muscles and a stern scowl. He was so powerful, with his large traps and biceps, that she didn't stand a chance of escape. At that realization, she gulped air and a little rain, choking on what could be her last breath.

When he dipped his head and spoke in her ear, she finally realized that he'd only pulled her close so she could hear him above the storm. "Do you know anything about guns?"

"I don't know. I don't remember." She swayed with the fear swelling up her throat as he took out a gun.

He pried open her fingers and placed the gun in her hand. The cold metal and unfamiliar feel of the grip set her hand to shaking. Stunned, confused, she tried to read the expression in his eyes, but the lightning refused to cooperate and flash. The wind kept roaring, blowing bits of sand that pinged against her exposed flesh and shredded her reasoning until she could barely read her own thoughts.

Again, he spoke into her ear. "Does holding this gun make you feel any safer?"

Why should it? She didn't know how to use it. However, as the weight settled in her hand, she finally realized that he'd given her the gun in an attempt to alleviate her fear. Her hand stopped shaking as some of her panic subsided.

When he leaned over this time to speak above the howling wind, she didn't automatically jerk back. He pointed to a little switch on the gun. "The gun won't

fire unless you flick the safety to the off position."
He demonstrated, then flicked the switch back.
"Once the safety is off, you only have to pull the
trigger and the gun will shoot. If I let you keep the
gun, will you ride with me on the bike? I need one
hand for the clutch, one for the throttle."

If she refused, what would he do? She really didn't
want to find out. Besides, while she knew he was
trying to stem her fears, she didn't want to seem like
a pushover. But she didn't want to tick him off by
remaining so suspicious when he so obviously
wanted her to believe him.

As her teeth chattered and her terror slowly subsided, she finally let him float his jacket over her
shoulders and placed the gun in the pocket. The
leather enclosed her in a cocoon of black warmth and
quiet heat. She liked the scent of the leather mixed
with his own spicy musk. "Where are we going?"

When they reached his bike, he said, "First, to find
you a doctor."

Melinda nodded in agreement. A doctor could
keep her safe—call the police and verify Clay's
story.

He placed an extra helmet on her head and donned
his own, revved the bike's engine and then helped
her sit behind him. He guided her feet to foot pegs,
and then, uncertainly, she wrapped her arms around
him. She couldn't reach completely around his huge
body, so she twisted her fingers through his heavy
leather belt.

As soon as they started down the beach, she realized that, due to their speed, his body sheltered her
from the worst of the elements. But wind whipped

at their already wet clothing, making her extra grateful for the protection of his jacket.

If he intended her harm, he wouldn't have given her his jacket, would he? Nor would he have insisted that she keep the gun.

Yet she couldn't help wondering if he'd made the gesture just to win her cooperation, to woo her into a false sense of security. As he smoothly drove off the beach and onto the road up the coast, she considered whether she should try to flee at the first red light.

She couldn't run faster than Clay on foot, never mind Clay on his bike. Deciding she had no choice but to stay with him for now, she vowed to focus on regaining her memory.

She studied the storefronts, hoping for a few more flashes, glimmers into her past that she believed had momentarily surfaced back on the beach. Nothing came to her until they passed a grocery store, the same chain where she shopped! She was sure of it, Just as she'd known when she'd run from Clay that if she could have made it to the water, she could swim. Somehow she knew she was an excellent swimmer, yet she had no concrete memory to pin her facts on.

She kept peering through the rain, wondering if she would recognize her house if she saw it. Her house? A picture of a tiny bungalow with a sagging roof and a cute mellow-yellow front porch with lots of hanging plants came to mind. She thought she lived there, maybe rented the house. She envisioned the cozy layout, two comfortable bedrooms divided by a bath, a small, friendly living room, a tidy but minuscule kitchen. She stored her windsailing equipment in the roomy shed out back and tried to think of a number on her mailbox or a street sign to help her figure out her address.

Nothing.

Frustrated, yet pleased that parts of her memory seemed to be returning, she tried to be patient. The man on the cycle in front of her caused another entirely new set of problems for her to consider as he repeatedly checked his rearview mirror as if expecting someone to follow them.

Did he watch so vigilantly for the police? Or the return of the two men he'd claimed had run her off the road?

Either scenario made her stomach churn with anxiety. If Clay feared the cops, then he was a bad guy. If he worried over the return of the two men, then someone had just tried to kill her.

As Melinda worried over whether or not to trust Clay Rogan, she felt the heavy gun weighing down her pocket and considered whether she could shoot someone and snuff out a life—for eternity. Without a lifetime of memories, she figured that her biggest handicap was that not only didn't she know if she could trust Clay, she didn't know if she could trust herself. She didn't know her own values. She didn't know if she voted Republican, Democratic or Independent. She didn't know how she'd react to danger, didn't know if she could aim the gun and pull the trigger—not even if her life depended on it.

CLAY SAW NO SIGN of pursuit. But no way could he relax or forget their pressing problems with Melinda pressed so tightly to him. Even through the leather jacket he'd given her to wear, he could feel her shivering on the seat behind him. So far he hadn't done such a hot job of protecting her, but now that he'd found her, he was determined that would change.

With the sky dark from horizon to horizon, rain teeming down in giant buckets and lightning occasionally striking nearby, the huge thunderstorm showed no signs of abating. Without a direct sign of pursuit, he couldn't justify fleeing with Melinda possibly still in shock and injured. She needed to be warm. Needed to see a doctor.

His first thought was taking off her wet clothes and heating her with his own body. But he shoved the inappropriate image aside almost immediately.

Instead he peered through the rain and spied a coffeehouse in one of those strip malls that included an ice-cream shop, a ladies boutique and a gift emporium. After parking the bike where it wouldn't be easily spotted, he took her icy hand in his. Guilt stabbed him for not taking better care of his charge. First she almost drowned, then almost froze to death. "Come on."

"Where're we going?" She spoke slowly between chattering teeth.

"To get you dry and warm."

He opened the boutique door and ushered her inside, hoping to be hit with a blast of warmth. But air-conditioning turned on cool made it seem as if they'd entered a refrigerator.

A middle-aged woman doing paperwork behind a desk took one look at his black leather jacket wrapped around a dripping-wet Melinda and frowned. "Can I help you?" she asked hesitantly, her soft Southern accent firm but polite.

Clay reached for his wallet and took out two hundred-dollar bills. "We got caught in the storm. The lady needs a towel and a new outfit to wear home."

The saleslady glanced from the cash to Melinda and her face brightened. "I have just the thing. You poor dear."

Ten minutes later, Clay had his soggy jacket back, and Melinda left the store wearing new navy stretch jeans and matching denim jacket over a red slinky top that showed an inch of skin at her flat stomach. Her teeth had finally stopped chattering, although her lips still held a tinge of blue. Clay noted the bulge in her jacket pocket and realized she'd transferred the gun to her new attire.

"I'll pay you back when I—"

"Don't worry about it." Clay held her elbow and escorted her toward the coffee shop. "How about a bowl of hot soup and some coffee?"

"Hot anything sounds good."

He knew she referred to the food, but his mind did a double take anyway. Such a sexually oriented thing—the male mind. He doubted she realized that while she'd changed clothes in the privacy of a cubicle and he'd stood guard, his mind had played all kinds of tricks on him. He'd imagined her peeling back her wet shirt and shorts to reveal very rounded curves. He'd wondered if she'd removed her wet underthings or kept them on. While it should have made no difference at all to him whether or not she still wore underwear, he couldn't help wondering whether he would be able to tell once she warmed up and removed her jacket.

He'd unintentionally brushed against her breasts too many times today not to be curious. Yet...while he knew his thoughts to be distracting and totally unprofessional, he had too much male in him to resist indulging in the fantasy. He'd wondered why he was so fascinated with her—he liked slim blondes, didn't he? But suddenly he realized that he'd been deceiving himself. Curvy brunettes had a lot to offer.

Idiot. She's not offering you anything.

They had the coffee shop to themselves, and Clay commandeered a booth near the foggy front window where he could watch the parking lot while they ate and talked. After the waitress took the orders, he could practically see the questions reflected in Melinda's topaz eyes.

"Why is the CIA interested in me?" she asked.

She might not have her memories, but her keen intelligence showed as she burned through the fog and fired to the heart of the matter. He drummed his fingers on the table. How much should he tell her? He was supposed to gain her trust before asking about the documents, and she certainly didn't trust him yet. In fact, he considered himself lucky that she hadn't tried to convince the saleslady or the waitress to call the cops.

"Since you've lost your memory, I'm going to have to explain some things to you before I answer your question."

She clasped her hands together and leaned forward. She'd done something to her hair, pulling it back from her face, smoothing it into a semblance of order. But water kept trickling from it, one suggestive droplet running down her neck and onto the thin red shirt.

He had to force his eyes to remain on her face and not follow the enticing direction the water had taken. "You have a brother and a sister, but after your parents died, the siblings were split up. Your older brother, Jake Cochran, grew up in foster homes and started looking for you the day he graduated from high school. Until recently, he couldn't find you. But then he uncovered copies of your birth certificates. The information led him to—"

Her eyes narrowed. "My own brother wants me dead?"

"On the contrary. Jake asked the government to protect you. So here I am." Clay gave her the simplified version of his story. While Jake had never asked the government to protect his sister, he had hired bodyguards for both sisters. Before Melinda's bodyguard could contact her, he'd been grievously wounded but had survived for several hours before he'd died. He'd used those hours to contact the director for help.

"And why does my brother think I need protection?"

"We're not sure."

"Why don't we call and ask him?"

"We suspect he's running for his own life right now."

"And my sister?"

"She has already gone underground."

The waitress returned and placed coffee cups and

steaming bowls of chowder in front of them. Melinda tasted her coffee and frowned.

"What's wrong?" Clay asked.

"Apparently I don't like coffee."

The waitress gave her an odd look.

"Could I have a hot chocolate instead?"

"You like hot chocolate?" Clay asked as he sipped his own black coffee.

"I'm not sure. The request slipped out before I thought about it."

"Have any of your memories returned?"

She shook her head, but he wasn't sure if she was telling the truth. "It's horrible, you know? The worst is not trusting...my own reactions." She looked at the soup in front of her as if it might bite her, then determinedly looked deep into her bowl. "I don't even know if I like clam chowder."

"There's one way to find out." Sensing her vulnerability, knowing she was hanging on to her dignity by just a few threads, he handed her the spoon.

She hesitated, then accepted the utensil. He figured she might take the tiniest taste, but she filled the spoon to the rim and took a full bite. "Mmm." She swallowed and scooped up more of the thick chowder. "Delicious."

"I know it must be frightening to have forgotten your past, but maybe you could look at it as an adventure—"

"Easy for you to say."

"Think of all the fun things you can learn all over again." Like kissing and making love and... Clay shut the thought down hard. He didn't like his mind drifting while he tried to make a point. He didn't need the distraction of thoughts about sex. He needed to keep his personal life separate from business, each segment neat and tidy in its own compartment to be taken out and savored at the right time. "Everything is a new experience for you. But maybe they'll be good experiences."

"Like when I rode a roller coaster for the first time. I was scared to death but it was a blast."

"You remember?" he asked, hopeful. He needed her memory to return as soon as possible. It was critical to recovering the documents her brother had sent her.

"I remember the wind in my face. My stomach swooping in fear. It was exhilarating—not the sickening fear I felt back on the beach."

If one memory had returned, maybe the others would follow. Clay told himself not to push her. He couldn't afford to scare her again. He needed her trust.

As MELINDA ATE, she wondered if Clay Rogan was playing her for a fool. But if he meant her harm, if he wasn't with the CIA, would he have been so concerned about her health? Ignoring his own discomfort, Clay had given her his jacket, and she suddenly realized how cold he must have been, riding in front and taking the brunt of the rain. Imagining the chill factor alone made her shiver.

He noticed immediately, his stormy green eyes narrowing with concern. "Eat some more soup."

"Yes, Mother," she teased, thinking the way he looked at her was anything but motherly. He maintained this rock-solid glint at all times, but even so, she discerned a hint of speculative interest there.

Interest in her?

At the thought, she almost dropped her spoon, just barely raised the soup to her mouth without making a total klutz of herself. Realizing that she wanted to trust him, she considered whether she'd believed him too easily. Lots of sickos wanted their women warm and healthy.

Yet every time she glanced into those direct eyes of his, she had trouble thinking of him as a pervert. It was like trying to imagine Clint Eastwood or Harrison Ford as a bad guy. She simply couldn't discern any evil in his hard, rugged features. On the other hand, she wasn't so naive that she didn't know looks could be deceiving.

Frustrated that she couldn't make up her mind, she shifted uneasily in her seat. Again those all-seeing green eyes noticed. "Something wrong?"

"I have to use the ladies' room." She stood. "Be back in a minute."

She left the table without asking his permission, wondering if he'd allow her to walk away. It took all her willpower not to look back over her shoulder at him, especially when she felt his stare drilling between her shoulder blades.

When she reached the ladies' room, she turned to enter and barely restrained a gasp. Clay was right behind her. How the huge man had moved so silently, she had no idea. But he'd followed, never letting her move more than two steps away from him.

Frightened and angry that he trusted her so little while he asked her to trust him with her life, she whirled around to confront him. Again he'd anticipated her reaction and was already pointing to the back door. "If those men found my bike, they could barge in and grab you," he explained.

"You aren't coming inside?"

He opened the ladies'-room door, glanced at the empty cubicles and the tiny window. Holding the door open for her, he leaned against the hallway wall, a satisfied look in his eyes. "I'll just wait here to make sure you make it back safely."

Without another word, she pushed through the doorway, her pulse still skittering. Was he really so concerned for her safety? Or did he fear she'd try to escape out the back door?

Thinking hard, she entered a stall, slipped out of her jacket and hung it on the hook. She took care of business, flushed the toilet, unlocked the door and reached for her jacket. The gun he'd given her fell out of the pocket to the floor with a clatter, skidding toward the sink.

She didn't think the gun could discharge like that. He'd told her it wouldn't fire with the safety on. Still, she found herself tensed and holding her breath. Finally when nothing untoward occurred, she leaned over and gently picked up the weapon.

Her thumb pressed something and she heard a faint click. The clip inside the handle slid out.

She started to shove the clip back into the gun. Her body turned icy.

The gun he'd given her to protect herself from him…had…no…bullets.

Chapter Three

Melinda gasped and swore at the sight of the clip that was as empty as her head was of memories. Clay had tricked her, making her believe she had a reliable weapon when in reality, if she'd pulled the trigger, nothing would have happened.

She should have been scared, but anger simmered through her veins, heating her face in embarrassment at buying his deception. How dared he play with her? Before she could decide her next move, Clay opened the rest-room door. "I heard a noise. You okay?"

"Damn you. No. I'm not okay." She held out the gun in one hand, the empty clip in the other, wishing she could throw it at his head without fear of retaliation. "You lied to me again."

"I didn't." He reclaimed his weapon and reholstered it somewhere behind his back as casually as if they were discussing whether she preferred coffee or hot chocolate.

"You may never have *said* the gun was loaded but you implied it."

He shrugged, male amusement glittering in his eyes. "I couldn't in good conscience give a loaded gun to a woman who doesn't know how to use it, now, could I?''

His amusement and logic irritated, like fingernails scratching a blackboard. "You don't have a conscience.''

"And you are making accusations without all the facts.'' He reached into his shirt pocket and extracted a Palm Pilot. "Here, I'm breaking the agency rules again, but I think you should read your file.''

Like she knew how to use it! She wasn't great with technical things. How did she know that? She refused to take the calculator-size gadget from him. "You could have typed anything in there. Why should I believe words on a screen any more than words from your mouth?''

He hesitated, his eyes searching hers and catching some of her frustration. "Why *shouldn't* you believe me?''

Again, he'd made a good point, but this time she could talk through the heat of her anger. "Can I phone a CIA office to verify your story?''

"That would jeopardize the security of the operation. As I told you, I'm working undercover.''

"Why?''

A waitress pushed through the door of the ladies' room and frowned at Clay. "Is there a problem here?''

"I thought she fell,'' Clay explained with a roguelike smile. "I just wanted to make sure she's all right.''

That he could have heard anything from the hallway that made him think she'd fallen pushed the boundary of common sense. It was much more likely

Clay had heard her gasp of surprise at the missing bullets, but the waitress bought his story, delivered with a sincerely apologetic but a virile I'm-a-man-and-must-protect-a-woman smile. Melinda made a mental note to remember he could lie and smile with charming candor at the same time.

Clay escorted her back to their table. While they finished their meal, he explained why she couldn't call the CIA. "The director thinks someone at the agency may be behind the operation against you."

She didn't understand. "Doesn't the director *know*? After all, he's the head of operations."

"It's a very large agency with thousands of employees."

"What are you saying? Exactly?"

"Sometimes factions occur in large organizations. Splits that lead to secret operations."

"You're talking about people with their own agendas within the CIA?"

"Their own *illegal* agendas."

Like murdering innocent citizens? "And what would they want with me?" She mopped up the last of her clam chowder with a hunk of thick bread and wondered if this story was any more true than the last lie he'd fed her.

"You may have information they need."

Sure she did.

She chuckled. She couldn't help it. Soon a full-bellied laugh worked up her throat and out of her mouth. The thought of someone trying to kill her for information when she couldn't even remember what she had for breakfast was insane.

Clay shook his head at her. "This is serious."

"I know." So why couldn't she stop laughing? She must be hysterical, the logical part of her mind whispered. But the emotional part needed release from the tension. She'd almost drowned. Now she had killers after her. And no memory. To top off her ridiculous predicament, the only person standing between her and the killers was a dangerous-looking hunk in black leather who rode a motorcycle like a professional and had an unsettling way of making her believe in him when all the facts said otherwise. No wonder she was losing it, laughing so hard her eyes brimmed with more tears.

Watching as if he expected her to shake apart into a thousand pieces, Clay patted her on the back. "You aren't going to start crying again, are you?"

She shook her head and clamped down hard on her laughter by holding her breath. A minute or so later, her laughter abated, but she couldn't control her edgy nerves or the prickly ball of heat in her gut as Clay watched her with concern.

"I'm okay now," she assured him, taking a sip of ice water and almost erupting into another spasm of laughter when she thought how ridiculous it was for *her* to be reassuring *him*. But she fought back the impulse.

"So your boss sent you to protect me?" she asked.

"That's part of my job."

"And the rest?"

"Will have to wait until your memory returns." He paid their bill, left a healthy tip and walked her to the rear exit of the coffee shop where he'd parked his bike.

She didn't like his refusing to say more. What was

he keeping from her? And why? Deciding to trust him had been difficult enough, and now he had her second-guessing herself. Did he need time to think up more plausible excuses, or did he feel it futile to confide in her until her memory returned?

The worst of the thunderstorm had passed, although dark clouds still blocked the sun, and the air was laden with a muggy humidity that made her clothes stick to her. In the parking lot, stray raindrops rippled oil in black puddles that reminded her of the giant gaps in her memory, gaps that made her so vulnerable. The gusting wind hadn't died down much, and she appreciated the luxury of dry, new clothes in the chilly air. Still, she was glad she'd left her damp underwear on beneath the clinging red blouse, especially since Clay's sharp eyes never seemed to miss anything. So she buttoned the denim jacket as Clay looked at her in speculation.

She raised her chin. "What?"

"I should get you to a doctor."

"Why do I hear a 'but' coming on?"

"Because I don't want to take you to a hospital. Too many questions," he explained before she could ask. "The more people who see us together, the easier it will be for your pursuers to find you."

His businesslike tone and his casual mention of danger sent a shiver icing down her spine that had nothing to do with her damp underwear, the chilly wind or the storm clouds still overhead. "We could separate to avoid being seen together."

Exasperation roughened his tone. "Is that what you want? You want me to abandon you to those guys who ran your car into the Atlantic?"

She looked into his stormy eyes and wondered if he was lying again. She suspected no matter what she said, no matter how much she protested, Clay had no intention of leaving her to face the danger alone. He would follow his own conscience and do what he thought best. He had too much honest determination in the set of his chin, too much stubbornness in his clever eyes, too much character in the slant of his cheekbones to abandon a woman in trouble.

She wondered if a man had ever before made her feel vulnerable, scared and yet oddly on-the-edge-of-her-seat wild at the same time. Maybe it was the direct look in his eyes or the way his eyebrows knitted together in concern, but she found herself believing his story. He wasn't faking his concern. "This is for real, isn't it?"

"Yes."

"Someone's really trying to kill me?"

"My boss seems to think so." From a compartment in his bike, he removed a chamois and dried water off the seat with clever hands that had long, strong fingers. He swiped the chrome with a few extra strokes, caressing each curve of the metal, stroking the hard edges and corners with a familiarity that told her he'd repeated this task many times. Finally, he wrung out the chamois and placed it back inside the compartment.

"You still want to hide me?"

"Yes." He swung his leg over the cycle and handed her a helmet while he put on his own. "But first we need to take you to a doctor."

She accepted the helmet, had trouble with the chin

snap and let him tip up her chin so he could fasten it for her. Their gazes locked and she suddenly felt as if she was falling. "I thought you said—"

"No hospitals. A local doctor's office would be best."

"Without an appointment?" He had to be kidding. He obviously didn't live around here, where a typical wait for a consultation took one to two hours—and that was just to get inside the examination room.

Leaving the details to him and wondering why she could remember trivia like the waiting time in a doctor's office and not the important facts about her life, she swung onto the back of the bike. As at ease with her decision to go with Clay as she was with her position behind him on the black leather seat, she placed her feet on the footrests. Melinda might not have her memory, but she still had her instincts—instincts that told her this man with his hard edges and tempestuous eyes would make a good protector.

Melinda twisted her fingers through Clay's belt and prayed she wasn't making the biggest mistake of her life.

CLAY NEEDED TO DITCH his Harley. The men back on the beach would have called for backup and would be searching the area by now. On his bike, he and Melinda were simply too conspicuous. He hoped that after he'd parked behind the coffee shop no one had found his bike, disabled the alarm and hidden a bug that would transmit a signal for a tail to follow them. Without a thorough inspection, he couldn't be sure they'd gotten away from any interested observers, but he refused to take additional time to search, not when Melinda had fought such a difficult battle deciding whether to trust him. He'd seen her eyes mirroring her indecision, and he felt relief that she'd decided to cooperate.

He needed to go to ground. Hide Melinda.

For the umpteenth time, Clay wished he knew more about who he was up against. It could be one handler and his entire cell. Or the operation against them could come from higher up; that meant different cells, satellite surveillance, wiretaps and local law enforcement's cooperation if the leader had enough authority. If the betrayal inside the agency rose high enough, whoever was in charge could bring in outsiders who would believe they were aiding a totally legitimate operation.

Clay would strategize differently against different opponents. A few renegades would be much easier to hide from than a well-organized, high-profile search. Pulling into traffic, hoping they could spare the time for a doctor's visit, Clay automatically watched for a tail. He saw nothing, but didn't let up on his scrutiny, relying on his prodigious memory to keep track of the seemingly random traffic around them.

One positive point: The two men who'd forced Melinda into the sea knew it was unlikely she had the documents on her. The men had probably intended to grab her and force her to take them to the documents. And if Melinda's pursuers reported in, they'd likely be told to follow, not kill, her in the hopes of obtaining the documents for themselves.

As much as Clay wanted to search her house for the documents, as much as he wanted to press Melinda for their location, he knew his first priority had to be the safety of the woman clinging so fiercely to his back. Papers might be valuable for the secrets they told. But her life was precious, too. She was too young to die in some thirty-year-old conspiracy, and he intended to ensure her safety.

However, her proximity was doing things to him. Unexpected things. Like making his pulse beat just a little faster. Making his adrenaline rush a little harder.

It must be the danger, Clay thought, and the complications that had set in within such a short time. He could never resist a good puzzle, and what could be more intriguing than a person with no memories?

Her amnesia was one humongous problem. He wanted to hide her and study the documents. But she had no memory of them. So while they waited for her mind to heal, their pursuers could steal the documents if they found them first.

While he didn't know if such a thing were possible, he wished a doctor could give her some kind of medicine to relax her enough for her to remember. His mission had become much more complicated in the last two hours. He felt equipped to deal with swift pursuit, the danger to their lives and even her amnesia, but it was his confusing reactions to her that had him white-knuckling the clutch. How could he be attracted to a woman who didn't know who she was?

Even with no memories, her core personality shined through. First off, she was smart and sensitive, using her eyes, ears and intellect to figure out as much as she could about an untenable situation. She evaluated everything he told her, and yet, in the end, she had to rely on her instincts.

She had good ones. He *was* on her side. He respected her fears and her gutsy decision to throw in her lot with him. Vowing not to disappoint her, he drove right past a three-story medical building. He wanted a smaller medical practice and kept his eyes peeled for a house that had been converted into an office building with a doctor's shingle hung out front.

When he didn't spy what he had in mind, he settled for a walk-in clinic—one of those anonymous places where the personnel frequently rotated and where it wouldn't be unusual for everyone in the waiting room to be strangers to one another as well as the doctors and nurses.

He parked his bike around back again, then signed Melinda in under an alias. The waiting room was full of senior citizens with various stages of the flu, a two-year-old with cheeks swollen like a chipmunk and a construction worker with a gash that looked as if he needed stitches.

An hour and a half later, Clay realized they'd wasted their time. At least Melinda didn't have a concussion, but the doctor had no solution for her memory loss. As they headed to Clay's bike, he suspected he was more disappointed over the news than Melinda. The doctor had recommended rest and told them that if her amnesia was due to the blow to her head, her memory could come back at any time. Or the amnesia could be caused by psychological trauma and her memory might take months to return—if it ever did.

So he knew little more than when they'd come in.

Had the delay given their pursuers time to spot them? Or call in their tag number to another team up the road?

He wouldn't take that chance.

A few miles down the highway, Clay found a motorcycle dealership across from a used-car lot. He paid the dealer to store his bike, and then he purchased a white midsize sedan with cash and a fake ID he had ready for such an occasion. Once they settled into the car, Clay missed the feel of her pressed to his back, and now, without the wind to drown out their conversation, he'd have to respond to her questions.

Only she didn't ask any. While she rested her head back against the seat and closed her eyes, he helped himself to a piece of cherry gum from his jacket pocket. The stress of the day had clearly caught up with her. Dark circles beneath her closed eyes and the weary tilt of her head told him she badly needed rest.

Her hair was dry for the first time since he'd found her on the beach, and it hung straight and shiny, framing her high cheekbones. Long bangs emphasized her wide-set eyes, which remained closed.

Where should he take her?

Clay had a hideaway prepared, a place where he could decode the documents and where it was unlikely they would be found. But he didn't want to compromise their location by going there more than once. Without the documents, he'd have to backtrack.

While he kept working through the puzzle, he kept driving.

MELINDA WASN'T TOO worried by the doctor's prognosis. Opening her eyes, she took in the scent of cherries and recognized the street Clay was driving on, knew if they made a right, they'd head toward the racetrack, and if they kept going straight, they'd eventually run into the interstate where they could head north toward Jacksonville, west toward Orlando or south toward Miami.

When Clay passed a local fast-food restaurant, she recalled eating French fries and drinking a chocolate shake with some people her age, who were wearing tank tops and shorts as if they'd just come from the beach. Yes, her memories were starting to return, but she kept that information to herself.

She glanced at the big man driving and realized how little she knew about him. He didn't look like a spy. At six and a half feet tall, she couldn't imagine him merging into a crowd and being unnoticeable. While he seemed competent and smart, she wanted to know more about him. "How did you come to join the CIA?"

"The agency recruited me right out of military intelligence. I went straight into military intelligence after college."

"What was your major in college?"

"Linguistics and mathematics, specifically logic."

"Really?" She couldn't keep the surprise out of her tone. Although she'd never attended college, she envisioned math students as short, nerdy guys with broken glasses taped at the nosepiece and plastic pocket protectors. "Why does the CIA need someone with your skills?"

"I'm into puzzles."

She frowned. "Like crossword puzzles?"

"I'm a cryptanalyst. My math skills come in handy when I break codes."

"I would have thought computers do that nowadays."

Clay turned right, heading north, methodically chewing his gum. "Computers can't think. They only process information. I program them and tell them how to think."

"O—kay. You just lost me." Or maybe it was watching his strong jaw chew that made it difficult to concentrate.

"Suppose someone from Cuba transmits a message to Russia. The computer can sort and analyze and translate much faster than a human brain—but it needs me to guide it, to think creatively. The computer needs directions."

She grinned. "And so do you. This road dead-ends up ahead. Make a left up there and—"

"Did your memory come back?"

She shook her head and he kept his face perfectly and carefully neutral. Melinda told herself she needed to be more careful. Clay noticed details. It had been a mistake to admit that she recognized their location. While she'd decided to trust Clay, she planned to keep a few secrets to herself until she could be absolutely sure he was really there to protect her. "I just know where I am. Like I know how to speak." She stretched her feet out and tried to change the subject. "Were you sent on this mission to decode something?"

"Let me back up and explain." Over the next fifteen minutes, Clay told her that her brother, Jake

Cochran, had sent her copies of papers that once belonged to her mother, that her mother had worked for the CIA and been murdered, and that the papers might have been written in code.

After listening to his explanation, she realized Clay wanted her to hand over those papers to him! While she couldn't remember the diaries or photographs or letters her brother had sent, strangely, she envisioned a cardboard envelope that had arrived in yesterday's mail, and she saw a label in dark, bold handwriting addressed to her. The return address had been from Jake Cochran. Now if only she could remember what she had done with the envelope. She suspected she hadn't opened it right away, because she couldn't recall the contents—that memory remained fuzzy like everything else that had happened this morning up to the time Clay had pulled her out of the sea.

Just as she'd become used to Clay's frequent glances in the rearview mirror and decided she had nothing to worry about, he scowled at the mirror and peeled sharply to the left. "Hold on."

Thankful for her shoulder harness, she braced one hand on the dash and peered over her shoulder. She saw a kid on a bike, several trucks and a bunch of cars. "What's wrong?"

"We're being followed."

She scowled into the mirror. "You sure?"

"See that gray car?"

"Yes."

"Watch."

Clay veered into the left lane and the car behind

followed suit. Then he pulled back into the right lane and turned right. So did the gray car.

Her stomach churned. "How did they find us?"

"Maybe we never lost them. Maybe they picked us up at the coffee shop or at the doctor's office."

"But you were careful."

"Look. These men are professionals. I assumed there were only a few of them, but they may have several teams. Or they called in reinforcements. Or one of us may have a bug on our clothes we don't even know about."

"I saw a movie where Will Smith had to remove his shoes and his belt buckle and ran away in his underwear."

"Let's hope it doesn't come to that."

"You have a plan?"

"I'm making it up as I go along."

"That's reassuring."

Clay sped through traffic while Melinda tried to fight down the churning in her gut. Five-o'clock rush hour was swiftly approaching, and she didn't know whether that was to their advantage or disadvantage. Clay couldn't drive as fast, but it might be easier to lose their pursuers in the traffic.

"There." She pointed. "Pull into that parking lot and around the back of the warehouse."

Without question, Clay followed her directions. The warehouse was a commercial site fronting the highway on one side and the intracoastal waterway on the other. The building hid them from the road, and if Clay had gained enough lead time, the gray car should drive right by.

Clay looked right and left. "We need to hide our

vehicle under something. If they have us pegged with satellite surveillance we're sunk.''

"Will a tiki hut work?'' She pointed to a hut with palm fronds over it. While the roof couldn't hide the entire vehicle, it hid the bulk of their car.

Clay parked, unsnapped his seat belt and unholstered his gun. "Come on.''

She slipped out of the car seat, hoping they wouldn't have to run far on foot. "Where?''

Before Clay could answer, the gray car pulled into the parking lot.

Chapter Four

At the sight of the gray car that he'd suspected had been tailing them, Clay grabbed Melinda's hand and pulled her around the opposite side of the building. They pressed against the dingy metal, listening over the buzz of mosquitoes, the occasional seagull diving for dinner and the hum of motorboats.

Out front, traffic on the busy two-lane highway served as background noise, trucks blowing their horns, brakes squealing and radios blaring. The peaceful lapping of the intracoastal waterway against the marshlands seemed to mock them. If the sedan followed them to the rear of the building, the occupants would spot their car under the tiki hut.

Beside him, Melinda's eyes grew big and her face paled, but she kept her composure, remaining silent, eyes alert. Clay thought he heard the car shift into Reverse, then pull back into traffic, but couldn't be certain.

"Wait here."

He edged around the building, gun out and ready to use if necessary, although he'd never fired in the line of duty. Clay bent low and peered around the building's rusted metal corner. At the sight of the empty lot, he stood and waited to make sure they were really gone.

Someone bumped into him from behind and his heart kicked into his ribs. He spun quickly, gun high, aiming right at...Melinda. "I told you to—"

"—wait." She scratched her chin. "I know. I know. But I don't like being left alone. It comes from my childhood."

"How so?" he asked casually, reholstering the gun, fully aware that she was starting to remember things and yet not openly admitting it. Her pretending caused him to feign a casualness he didn't feel. Her reluctance to admit to her returning memory bothered him on several levels. He didn't like liars, but more importantly, he needed her to trust him. Yet, clearly, Melinda Murphy wanted to hold on to some secrets while apparently willing to share others.

"Before my folks divorced, things were bad at home." Her voice stayed even, low and slightly sad.

They walked to the car and Clay started the engine, but he didn't pull out of the lot. Better to let the search on the road pass him by before he poked his head out.

"Did your father abuse your mother?" he asked, curious to see how far her memories would take her. He found it odd that she didn't seem to notice that she could now recall things about her life that she couldn't earlier. But then he supposed memories could be tricky things. Sometimes senior citizens could more easily remember an incident that happened forty years ago than a movie they'd seen last week.

"My mother wouldn't have tolerated violence. But what my father did to her was almost as bad."

Clay frowned, not sure he wanted to hear this but needing to encourage any memories at all. "What did he do?"

"It sounds like such a little thing. But it wasn't. Not to my mother. You see, my dad was a traveling salesman. Sometimes he sold bibles, other times vacuum cleaners or phone cards or service plans for computers. He was on the road a lot and didn't come home on a regular basis. The separation was hard on their marriage."

"And?"

"And he broke my mother's heart. He'd tell her he would be home for Thanksgiving and she'd cook and clean and buy a new dress and…he wouldn't show. Then she'd try to hide her tears from me, but I always knew her red eyes were from crying. Maybe because I'd been crying, too."

"Was he cheating? Drinking?"

She shrugged. "I don't really know."

"The man had to earn a living." Clay couldn't help defending her dad, more to see what else she would say than because he believed her father had been in the right.

"But he didn't have to hurt her so much. Mom never talked about him after the divorce."

"Did she remarry?"

"No, and we never again saw my father after I was five."

This memory was very specific. "You're sure it was when you were five?"

"He'd missed Thanksgiving and Christmas. It was

my birthday in February. He actually made it home that time. He brought me a doll. Mom handed him divorce papers. We never saw him again.''

"I'm sorry."

She shrugged. "It was a long time ago."

"What else can you remember?"

"That's it. The memory just popped whole into my head. As if I dreamed it. But it was real."

"How can you tell?"

"I'm not sure." She frowned at him. "Do you remember your dreams?"

"Sometimes."

"Can you tell me the difference between the memory from your dream and the memory of an actual event from your life?"

He knew what she meant. Of course, he knew the difference. Everyone did. Yet he was at a loss to explain the difference with words.

"We should go to my house," she suggested suddenly, her tone rising with excitement.

"You remember where you live?"

"I see the house in my head. It's wooden and yellow and has a front porch. I don't know the address. Don't you have it on file?"

"Sure, but—"

"Maybe in familiar surroundings my memories will come back."

She might be right. "It will be dangerous to go there."

"It's dangerous here." With her fingers, she combed her bangs back from her eyes and looked straight into his with an intensity that showed she was set on convincing him. "I might have a pet that needs feeding. Messages on an answering machine to return. My mother might be worried about me."

"I don't think so."

"Why not?"

Damn. He hated giving her bad news. "I'm sorry. She died last year. Heart attack. Your file says she went to sleep and never woke up." As if telling her that her mother hadn't suffered could make her feel better. She seemed all alone in this world.

"Take me home, Clay. You need me to go there anyway since that's where I left the papers my brother Jake sent me, right?"

"You remember them?"

"I remember the envelope they came in. My brother used a black marker and addressed the package with a bold scrawl. But I have no recollection of the package's contents."

"Or where you put them?"

"Or where I put them," she agreed. "However, if we go back to the house, I'm hoping I'll remember. Or maybe we'll just find them."

"You sure you want to risk it? Why don't you let me stash you someplace safe and search your house alone? That way, if anyone is waiting with any unpleasant surprises, at least you won't be in danger."

She shook her head. "How long do you think I'd last, alone, fleeing from the CIA? Come on. I might as well go with you and let them get me now as opposed to later."

For a woman who didn't have many memories, she sure seemed to know what she wanted. Her rationale did follow a certain kind of twisted logic.

Still, he hesitated. "It's likely someone is waiting to grab you at your house."

"Maybe we should call the cops and have them meet us. Wouldn't there be safety in numbers?"

"Maybe. Maybe not." He considered her suggestion. "On one hand, I'd welcome the backup—just to keep you safe. But if our opponents guess our plan, they can pretend to be on legitimate agency business and ask the cops to hand us over to them."

"Would the police do that?"

"It depends." With the sun setting and slashing the sky with purples and pinks, Clay finally pulled out of the parking lot.

"Depends on what?"

"On how well the head of the local cell knows the chief of police. Or if the agency has worked with the cops down here and if they've stepped on any toes."

"In other words...you have no idea."

"I'm giving you possibilities."

"Based on pure conjecture."

"And experience."

"Well, unless you have a better suggestion, I vote you take me home."

MELINDA'S MEMORIES SEEMED to be a patchwork blanket. Some recollections came back whole, some in tiny bits and pieces. Some came without effort, while others persisted on being tucked away and remaining secret and hidden behind a wall of darkness. While part of her last week was clear, today still seemed very fuzzy.

While she could recall the house where she lived

quite clearly and had no trouble directing Clay there, she couldn't recall her address. Yet she pictured the cozy house at the far end of a neighborhood with ease. Right now she treated clients in her spare bedroom, which she'd fixed up for massage therapy. Soon she'd have enough money saved to start up her dream salon, a full-service business in a wealthy area where she could draw an affluent clientele.

Her goal of owning her own business, the building that housed it and the land on which it was located would happen soon. She would close on the land, give the contractor a down payment and order the expensive equipment needed to make the posh salon appeal to the wealthy. She'd saved and worked hard for this opportunity and she wasn't about to let the surprise from her past ruin the future she'd worked so hard to attain.

Melinda had learned the hard way that every woman should be able to support herself. After her parents' marriage had failed, her mother had struggled to keep a roof over their heads. While Melinda had never gone hungry, she often had no more to eat than a free school lunch and peanut butter and jelly sandwiches for dinner.

Melinda didn't care about being rich. What she'd worked so hard to attain was security. She wanted to know she could pay her bills. She wanted to know she could never be fired. Creating the salon was her way of banishing her past.

For now, she worked out of her leased home, content to live and work and save. She prayed the memories would keep flowing back, welcoming the bad parts in her past along with the good. She was anxious to see whether her newfound memories matched reality as they pulled up into her own driveway.

Clay—being Clay—didn't drive straight up to her home without making thorough preparations. He surprised her and used his cell phone to call the police, telling them mostly the truth—that she'd been attacked today on the beach, lost her purse and feared the muggers might be inside her home. He left out who he worked for and why he was with her. While the cops didn't appreciate her failure to report the incident on the beach, after Clay told them she'd now willingly file a complaint, they'd dispatched a squad car.

However, Clay still didn't approach her home without a backup plan of escape just in case things didn't go their way. After driving past her house twice, he parked one block north of her yard, and they strolled past her house once before he was satisfied that no one lurked, ready to pounce the moment they walked up her sidewalk. Still, he wouldn't let her go inside until after the police arrived.

The policemen parked in her driveway and introduced themselves as Officers Kevin Conley and Deke Jurgens. Officer Conley stayed with them while Jurgens inspected the outside premises.

After taking their statements, Officer Conley insisted on checking inside while Melinda and Clay waited under the granddaddy oaks that shaded her wide front porch. Too nervous to sit on any of the comfy furniture, she paced. Finally, Conley signaled that inside was safe and she stepped over the threshold.

The tidy two-bedroom bungalow stood neatly,

much as she had left it, with the quiet yellow curtains swaying over the screened windows, welcoming her home. Her furniture might have been bought at garage sales, the appliances old, but she enjoyed living here at the far end of this quiet neighborhood where people minded their own business and raised their children with small-town values. Her plants, huge ferns in ceramic pots, a few orchids about to bloom and several trays of herbs, looked undisturbed. Her house hadn't been trashed or damaged. From the neatly stacked china behind the glass doors of her cabinets, to her mustache cup collection, nothing looked out of place. The photographs on the wall of her windsailing and her neat stack of magazines on the coffee table looked untouched.

Yet, the hair on the back of her neck prickled. One picture was crooked. Very crooked. But it was more than just one off-kilter picture that made her heart pound against her ribs and caused her to feel violated.

Clay must have guessed from her expression that something was off. "What's wrong?"

The front rug over the hardwood floor was too close to the door and would jam it. She never left her jacket hooked over the doorknob by the hood, but by the neckline. She fought to keep her voice calm. "Someone's been here."

"Is anything missing, ma'am?" Officer Conley asked as he took out a notebook, clearly ready to write a report. Jurgens had rejoined them and looked around warily.

Melinda didn't want to tell them about her amnesia just yet and kept her reply vague. "I'm not sure."

"Where do you keep your mail?" Clay asked, seemingly uninterested in anything but retrieving the missing documents her brother had sent.

"I don't have a set place for the mail. Sometimes I dump it on the kitchen table. Or on my nightstand in the bedroom. Or on my desk in the therapy room."

"Therapy room?" Conley asked, looking up from his notes but continuing to write.

"I'm a massage therapist. Since my house fronts commercial property on the corner, building and zoning allows clients to come here."

"Could a client have disturbed your things?"

She shook her head, positive no client had been in her private area. "There's a separate side entrance and they only use that one room."

Clay methodically searched the kitchen countertops, then ducked into her bedroom. His gaze swept over her nightstands before he followed her into the therapy room. Her massage table dominated the twelve-by-twelve room. Massage oils, extra sheets and clean towels stood ready for her clients next to her desk, which held a message machine and a CD player.

She'd had a busy day yesterday, two clients in the morning, then three in the afternoon. While Melinda couldn't recall this morning, she knew all she had to do was check her day planner and her appointments would be listed.

She glanced toward her mahogany rolltop desk and hurried over. "My appointment book's gone."

"I doubt someone would steal that," Conley said. "Maybe you misplaced it."

She frowned, knowing that he didn't understand

how meticulous she was about keeping her appointments straight. "I always leave the book right by the phone. It's gone."

"All the same, would you mind checking the desk drawers?" the officer suggested.

Melinda did as he asked, knowing the search would prove fruitless. She always, always, always left her book and pen right there so she wouldn't get confused about her appointments. Without her book, she couldn't even call her clients to cancel their massage appointments tomorrow. "Who would want my schedule?"

"Someone who wanted to find you might look in there," Clay suggested. "Did you write that you planned to go to the beach today?"

"I doubt it." She blew her bangs out of her eyes in exasperation. "I only schedule work." Out of habit, she hit the play button on her answering machine. The machine clicked oddly as if the tape was stuck. Lifting the clear panel, she expected to find the cartridge. It was gone. "They stole my tape cartridge. I wonder if Jake tried to call?"

"Nothing else is missing?" Conley asked. "Money? Jewelry? Electronic equipment?"

Before she could answer, Clay spoke up. "The mail is gone, too."

"What's so important about her mail?"

"We think that's why she was attacked on the beach today," Clay explained, then proceeded to tell Conley about the incident on the beach earlier while his partner again went outside to check to see if the neighbors had seen or heard anything unusual.

Conley finished his report by the time his partner,

who'd learned nothing new, had returned. Conley wrote down Clay's cell phone number and promised to get back to them if anything turned up. Then, after presenting cards with their numbers to call if new troubles arose, both officers departed.

"How much can you remember?" Clay asked Melinda once they were alone again.

The house seemed more intimate with only the two of them. While Clay was a large man, he didn't dominate the space around him so much as fit into it. He seemed as comfortable inside her house as he had on his Harley, and she liked that about him. He wasn't stiff, but made himself at ease in her home as if he'd always been there.

"I've got almost everything back now." She saw no reason to lie to Clay anymore. "Except for the accident on the beach and the earlier part of the day, I seem to have recovered most, if not all, of my memories." She slumped on her couch. "Those guys who attacked me must have come here and stolen the package Jake sent me yesterday."

"Yesterday?"

"I remember it arriving yesterday and putting it by the phone. I'd scheduled two appointments and probably didn't open it until this morning."

"Which you still don't remember?"

She nodded. "But if that's what they were after, I'm safe now."

"Not necessarily." Clay took the chair opposite her. "They might still come back."

"But why? They have the envelope." She fought to keep disappointment from her face and a whine from her tone.

"People in this business like to tie up all the loose ends." Clay leaned toward her. "You'll be safer if you don't spend the night here."

His expression indicated that his mind was working at top speed. She assumed that he was analyzing every possibility like a chess master before making a move.

"What are you thinking?" she asked, wondering if she really wanted to spend the night alone, but figuring he wouldn't let her.

"I'm thinking it'll probably be useless to have a crime team come in and search for fingerprints. These guys are pros and know to wear gloves. But if they left a clue behind, maybe I could track them down and recover the items Jake sent."

He wanted to steal back the envelope from the rogue agents? She tried to keep the skepticism from her tone. "Is that possible?"

"Yeah, but unlikely since they didn't leave us any bread crumbs to follow."

"You're just giving up?"

He shot her a look hot enough to melt steel. "I didn't say that. First of all, we don't know for sure that the documents were stolen."

"But they aren't here."

"Maybe you misplaced them."

Melinda propped her feet up and considered his suggestion. "I suppose that's possible."

"But unlikely," Clay admitted while he stood and paced. "Our best bet is to track the men who were after you."

Melinda frowned at him in confusion. "But you just said they probably didn't leave any clues."

"Their being here tells me a lot."

"Like?"

"If these people work inside the agency, they probably obtained travel documents to fly here."

Melinda caught on immediately. "Who makes the travel arrangements at the CIA? If we could find out, we could figure out what names they are using and maybe track them—"

Clay chuckled at her enthusiasm. "Whoa! What's this *we* business?"

Melinda raised her chin. "It's my things they stole."

"Mmm."

She could tell he wasn't about to debate whether to allow her in on his plans. She found his attitude more than irritating. She wasn't about to let him stuff her in some safe house while he tracked down the bad guys. For one thing, she'd probably go stir-crazy wondering what was going on. Plus, she figured the safest place for her was right next to Clay.

It had nothing to do with his good looks. She felt safe with him. His sheer size should intimidate the enemy. He carried a gun. He was trained to deal with this cloak-and-dagger work. She was not interested in him, she told herself, trying to remember if she'd ever felt this comfortable with a man in her living room. She tended to say goodbye at the front door, rarely inviting a date into her personal space.

"Who made your travel arrangements?" she asked, going back to the subject at hand.

"I drove down, but if we get lucky, these guys might have flown." Clay hesitated, then swung a chair around and straddled it. "I can pull a string or two through the accounting department without raising any eyebrows to see if the agency paid for airline tickets to Daytona. Luckily, it's a small airport.''

She hated to dampen his enthusiasm but felt compelled to point out, ''They could have flown into Jacksonville or Orlando.''

''Or driven or taken the bus,'' he agreed. ''But it's unlikely.'' Clay took his cell phone from his pocket and punched in a series of numbers, then he punched in more numbers, and then more numbers.

She raised her eyebrows and he finally explained. ''My phone is scrambled, but, just in case anyone's interested in my conversation, I rerouted the call through a Canadian satellite.''

Clay didn't hide his end of the phone conversation from her, but she paid no attention to the technical jargon or the codes he rattled off as easily as she could recite the alphabet. Instead, she wondered if she was making a mistake sticking by him.

From their conversation, she knew he intended to hunt the men hunting her. Dangerous? Oh, yes. But would it be more dangerous than staying in her house like a sitting duck and waiting to see if those men returned to shoot at her? She squared her shoulders just as Clay finished his call and pulled out his Palm Pilot.

''The accountant downloaded the information to me and since it's wireless, it's untraceable.'' He pressed some buttons and two men's faces appeared on the screen.

The screen identified the first man as Victor Korbut. He was big, tough and mean-looking, with dark, bushy eyebrows that formed one solid line across the bridge of his oft-broken nose. The name under the second man's picture was Peter Price. He had sickly white acne-scarred skin, dirty-blond hair and aviator sunglasses.

Clay held the screen up to her. "You remember seeing these men?"

"No. Sorry."

"They flew into Daytona airport yesterday, rented a car and are staying at the Daytona Vacation Inn."

"You got all that information from accounting?"

"Sure. Agency employees have to fill out expense account forms just like everyone else."

Melinda didn't know what to make of the information Clay had just found with a simple phone call. She speculated on what he would do next. Find the other agents and confront them? Call in for backup? She didn't have a clue. She only knew that the look in Clay's green eyes had turned frosty, and she wouldn't want him aiming all that intellect in her direction if he was angry.

"Now what?" she asked.

"My mission is to decode the documents. I can't accomplish that without those pages. So—"

"We're going to steal them back?"

He shot her a cocky grin that warmed her straight through to her gut. "How do you feel about spying on our spies?"

Chapter Five

Clay didn't like taking Melinda with him, but by his calculations, the danger should be minimal. Leaving her alone wasn't an option he considered for long, not with so much of the puzzle still unsolved.

He wished he knew for certain whether the rogue CIA agents had stolen the documents or whether Melinda had simply misplaced them. Vowing to find out the answer quickly, he told Melinda to pack a few items of clothing and toilet articles since he had no idea when they would return.

The helpful accountant at the agency had told Clay the agents were checked into rooms 304 and 306 at the Daytona Vacation Inn. Clay made reservations and specifically asked for rooms 302 and 308 and lucked out that they were empty.

Melinda locked up her house. He carried her bag to the car parked one block away. Her neighborhood seemed normal for the dinner hour. Men and women came home from work and parked in their garages. Kids played basketball in their driveways. A dog down the street barked at a cat that had climbed onto a car roof.

"What's the plan?" Melinda asked him.

"My primary objective is still to keep you safe. Once we arrive, you are not to show your face."

She looked down at his size-fourteen feet and then up to the top of his full six-and-a-half-foot height and teased, "You're not exactly capable of being inconspicuous."

"That's why my plan is to hide. We wait until they leave their rooms to eat, then I raid the premises."

"*We* raid the premises." When he halted on the sidewalk, she stopped, too. She knew he didn't want her tagging along. "Look, it's my personal planner and my messages on that tape. While I'm sure you can find them on your own, don't you think I'd be safer right next to you than alone?"

"No, I didn't think of it." He hesitated to contemplate her words. "But after considering your suggestion, I still think you'd be safer staying hidden."

"Look, if you don't get caught snooping, it won't matter whether I'm with you. But if you do get caught, I won't stand a chance on my own. They'll simply come after me."

"You should have joined a debate team. Or become an attorney. Are you sure you're really a massage therapist?"

"Did Mr. Logic find my argument sound?"

Mr. Logic? Amusement deepened his tone. "You might be smart, but you can be a difficult partner."

"Partner? Is that your way of telling me I can come along?"

"I also called you difficult."

She seemed to take that as some kind of left-

handed compliment and grinned up at him, then
shrugged. "Every relationship has its problems."

Relationship. Whoa. She needed to slow her horse
down. They didn't have a relationship. They barely
had a working partnership. Then moonlight glinted
and he saw the laughter glimmering in her eyes and
realized she was teasing him. Again. In a way he
found downright disturbing.

Clay didn't want to think of Melinda Murphy as
a woman. She was an assignment. Unfortunately, she
was all woman *and* his assignment. A combination
he should have realized earlier would prove trouble-
some, especially since he tended to have workaholic
tendencies. Since she was part of his work, he supposed it was natural to have his thoughts all wrapped
around her. So why was he the one that felt smothered? And way too hot?

He had nothing to offer a woman like Melinda
Murphy, who had big plans for a stable future. After
the story she'd told him about her parents' breakup,
he figured she had no use for a man who lived for
his work.

Sure, he had hobbies like riding his Harley, but he
considered biking a solitary hobby—or at least he
had until he recalled the way she'd clung to him, her
thighs wrapped around him. He took a mental step
back. He didn't want a relationship with Melinda. He
wanted sex. Hot lusty sex—with no strings attached
in the morning.

But he already knew she wasn't that kind of
woman. She'd put down roots wherever she lived,
making her place her own. Even in a house she
leased, she had carefully matched the curtains to the

pillows on the couch, owned plants that took daily loving care, and had started a vegetable garden out back. She obviously possessed a deep nesting instinct, no doubt a by-product of her insecure childhood.

Taking her to bed wasn't an option—not for a man who didn't want attachments. But knowing the facts and seeing the pieces clearly in his head didn't make the lower parts of his anatomy any less restless.

Glad for the darkness that covered his state of semi-arousal during their confrontation, he continued to walk toward the car. She smelled good and her light step beside him had him very aware of the way she moved. He wondered how the hell he would sleep tonight with her in the same hotel room?

He recalled all those old movies where a couple showed up to find only one room and one bed. Here he already had two hotel rooms reserved but had to keep her with him all night to protect her.

"You've grown quiet," she commented as he placed her bag into the trunk.

"Just thinking."

"About?" she prodded.

"I don't want anyone to see you. That means while I register for the rooms, you stay in the car. I'll figure out a way to smuggle you up to the third floor after I check out the stairways."

"Okay."

She really could be quite reasonable when she set her mind to it. But he was still gritting his teeth against his reactions to her. He found her attractive when she fought him. He found her attractive when she agreed with him. He found her attractive when she just breathed.

He opened her door for her and she slid into the passenger seat of the car. "Can we stop somewhere for dinner?"

"I'm hoping to catch the men out of the room while they eat."

He heard her stomach growl as he closed her door and realized she'd eaten little for lunch—just a bowl of soup and a hunk of bread. He walked around to the driver's side and sat behind the wheel. "We could hit a drive-thru someplace. How about a burger and fries?"

"And a chocolate shake?"

He started the engine, drove down the street and merged onto the highway. "What is it about women and chocolate?"

She cocked her head. "You mean you have time in your life for something besides work and your bike? There's actually been a woman?" she teased. "Are you living with someone?"

"Never again."

"Again?"

"I was married once. It didn't work out."

"I'm sorry. Did you have kids?"

He frowned. "According to my ex, I wasn't home enough to make them."

He didn't like talking about his divorce. His wife had been a good woman, and he'd let her down by putting his work first. There was only one reason he was willing to tell Melinda about his past—so she'd realize she couldn't possibly have any kind of future with him.

"Do you know how to get to the Daytona Vacation Inn?" he asked at the stoplight, not only to confirm the directions on his Palm Pilot but to change the subject.

"Turn left and then right after two lights. It's across the street from the beachfront."

"You have any makeup in your purse?"

At the sudden change in topic, she twisted in her seat to look at him. "Why?"

"I'm hoping that the men on the beach didn't get a good look at me or you. While I'm going to do my best to avoid them at the hotel, anything you can do to change your appearance might help give us an edge if we do run into them."

While he drove into a fast-food restaurant line and ordered through his window, Melinda pulled out a brush and swept her hair up onto her head, then fastened it with some kind of hair gadget. She flipped down the visor of the mirror and applied so much eye makeup that he wanted to wash her face. But he could hardly complain after he'd asked her to do it.

He handed her the food without comment. She looked more sophisticated, older, wiser and way too sexy. Right now he needed more than a burger, fries and a soft drink to keep from thinking how good she looked. With her hair off her face, he could see her graceful neck and earlobes with tantalizingly tiny gold rings.

Forcing his eyes to his food, he ate quickly and stuffed the extra papers into the bag the food had come in. He sucked down his drink and let her finish eating before speaking. "In the back seat you'll find a briefcase. Open it and take out the two walkie-talkies."

She found them without trouble, and he explained to her how to turn the volume down to practically zilch and hold down the talk button, then release it to send a warning signal without speaking. "I'll register in the lobby while you wait in the car. Don't turn on any interior lights, and if you spot the men I showed you on the Palm Pilot, signal me."

"Are you going to give me a weapon?" she asked. Her voice was even, but he could see her neck strain with tension.

He shook his head. "Weapons are dangerous if you don't know how to use them." He pulled over into the hotel parking lot and turned in his seat to face her. "I don't expect to run into trouble, but if you want to back out, now's the time."

She didn't say a word for several long breaths, and he respected the fact that she was smart enough to consider the danger. Finally, she squared her shoulders and looked him straight in the eyes. "I'm good to go."

MELINDA MEANT THE WORDS she'd spoken. She didn't want to hide. Didn't want to be left behind. She'd feel safer with Clay and in the middle of the action than she would alone.

Clay hadn't parked directly in front of the lobby where the light shined brightly. Instead, he'd found a parking spot close to the door, but in relative darkness.

He performed one last radio check. "Lock the doors after I'm gone."

"Okay."

For a moment, she had the strongest feeling that he wanted to lean over and kiss her. Breathless, balanced between keeping still and falling over the edge, she let him make the decision to come closer. But he didn't and then he slid out of the seat. "I'll be right back."

Melinda realized this was the first time all day that he'd left her alone, and all she could think about was what it might have been like if he had kissed her. He'd be gentle and strong. And she imagined her heart doing cartwheels. Since not less than an hour ago he'd told her he was a divorced man who clearly wasn't interested in her, his slight hesitation before he left must have been wishful thinking on her part.

Fear must be doing strange things to her mind. This was the first time he'd left her unprotected since the incident on the beach—which she still couldn't remember. But she could remember her fright. Could still recall her heart pounding and her adrenaline pumping.

Now, in the dark shadows of the parking lot, without his presence, she felt more vulnerable—even with him only one walkie-talkie click away. During their day together she'd become accustomed to his nearness. The solid width of his shoulders made her feel protected, and so did the way he always considered her safety as his primary goal.

She also appreciated the fact that he intended to remain hidden during most of this entire assignment. That alone assured her he wasn't some hot dog full of testosterone and itching for a brawl. Clay preferred to use his brains rather than his brawn, and she appreciated that about him. She also liked the way he'd given her an out without making her feel like some silly woman who didn't know her own mind.

While she waited in the car, she tried to distract herself, watching the other vehicles pull in and out of the parking lot. She saw families go through the hotel lobby, saw a man slide into a taxi and a man and a woman pull up in different cars, go into one room and start kissing before they'd even shut the door. Were they a couple having an adulterous affair? A one-night stand after a pickup at a local bar? Or married and meeting halfway between different job locations?

Clay returned without her spying any men who matched the images she'd seen on his tiny computer screen. "Any problems?"

She shook her head. "What about you? You see them?"

"No." He held up two keys. "We'll drive around back and take the stairs instead of the elevator."

Once again, he parked the car, this time backing into the space as if he expected to have to make a fast getaway. She licked her lips and told herself he just wanted to be prepared.

Clay opened the trunk and took out her bag. She expected him to carry it for her again, but he held it out to her with another case that belonged to him. "Would you mind bringing these up? I'd prefer to keep my hands free."

"No problem." She slung the straps over her shoulder and tried to keep her pulse steady as he led the way. Although he went first, he still held open the door behind him for her.

There was nothing casual about his actions, which made her note his every movement in the bright lights of the stairwell. Clay's eyes scanned from side to side as he advanced up the stairs. His long legs could have easily taken the steps two at a time, but he didn't rush, waiting for her, never leaving her side. They passed no one.

When they reached the third floor, he motioned her back and ducked his head into the hallway. "It's clear. Once we're in the hall, if anyone comes by, face the nearest door, give them your back and pretend to be searching for your key."

"Got it." His precautions were making her breath come in ragged gulps.

By the time they arrived safely in one of the rooms he'd reserved, perspiration had beaded on her upper lip, and she felt as though she'd just accomplished a major feat. Never before had she realized that sheer tension alone could wear her out.

The tense situation hadn't appeared to faze Clay. He took his bag from her, opened it and pulled out some electronic equipment. With a suction cup, he stuck a wire with a tiny microphone attached to the wall between their room and one the agency's men occupied.

After several minutes, Clay unplugged the device. "I didn't hear anything."

"Maybe they're sleeping?"

Clay shook his head. "This microphone is sensitive enough to pick up the slightest sound. No one's in that room." He took the headset off and snapped open a box filled with sharp tools.

Her eyes widened. "You're going to pick the lock?"

"The one on the balcony."

"Why can't you pick the lock in the hallway?"

"I could. But we're much more likely to be spotted out there by another hotel guest, a bellhop or maid."

She supposed that made sense, although the balconies exposed them, too. The rooms on this side of the building all had terraces with ironwork railings. Climbing from theirs to the one next door shouldn't be difficult if she could forget they were three stories off the ground. While Melinda didn't particularly enjoy heights, she didn't have any abnormal fears of them, either. Yet her pulse escalated as she realized that a three-story fall had to be high enough to kill.

Clay extracted from his pocket two pairs of thin rubber gloves like those a surgeon might use, and handed her a set. "Put these on."

She thought the gloves would make them conspicuous or clumsy. After donning them, she realized how close someone would have to look at the skin-toned, thin material to see that it wasn't her real skin. And after a minute or two, she actually forgot they were on her hands.

"You can stay here," Clay offered again.

"I'd rather climb over the balcony with you."

"In that case—" Clay flipped off the room's interior lights "—let's go."

MELINDA DIDN'T KNOW which was worse, watching Clay climb over the balcony or doing it herself. Physically, the maneuver wasn't that difficult, especially with Clay lending her a steadying hand. However, if the rusty railing they clung to broke loose, or if she lost her balance and pulled Clay with her, they'd both be goners.

She covered the last bit of distance by holding her breath and telling herself that Clay wouldn't let her fall. Finally, her feet touched solid concrete on the other balcony. She tried not to think about climbing over again to search the second room if they didn't find the missing documents here.

Clay took out a penlight, and within moments he'd successfully jimmied the lock to the agents' room. He opened the door, and the cool air-conditioning struck her in the face and reminded her to breathe.

Clay went in first and she stayed close behind, shutting the glass door behind them. Quickly he shined the light over the bed and nightstands. He moved to the dresser drawers, opened each one, rifled through the clothes, then slowly and soundlessly shut them to go on to the next.

She pointed to the closet where several suits hung. While Clay checked the shelf, she dug into the jacket pockets. She found loose change, a clean handkerchief and breath mints. Something hard and plastic rubbed her fingers. Something rectangular.

In the darkness, she pulled out the object. "Clay?" she whispered. "I found something."

He shined the light on her hand. She held the missing tape to her answering machine.

"Good work."

Clay's praise didn't stop her hand from trembling with both fear and excitement. Hoping the men hadn't erased her messages, she slipped the tape into her pocket. Her find told them several things. The men who'd paid for this hotel room were the same men who had been inside her house. Not only that, but she and Clay now had proof that what his boss had suspected was true. These men were running their own illegal operation from within the CIA.

Still searching for the missing papers her brother had sent her, Clay checked under the bed, inside the medicine chest and behind several pictures that hung on the wall. He even tilted the mattress and box spring off the bed before neatly smoothing everything back the way it was.

The room had yielded all the information it held.

Once again, Clay took the microphone and headset out and attached them to the wall of the second room. While he listened, her nerves stretched taut. If the men returned, they'd be caught red-handed with the tape. But she couldn't complain. She'd asked to come with him and refused to let her rising fears interfere with his mission.

He motioned her back toward the balcony, opened the door, and they both exited the room. This time not only did they have to cross from one balcony to the next, they had to navigate around a concrete structural pillar.

Again, Clay picked the lock within seconds. While she fervently hoped she'd find her appointment book or the information her brother had sent, this room was empty except for furniture and men's clothing.

Clay had just about finished his methodical search when she heard footsteps down the hall. Clay grabbed her hand and yanked her toward the balcony.

As someone clicked a key card into the hallway door's lock, Clay shut the balcony door behind them.

Hearing footsteps enter the room, they stood on the terrace with only a glass door and a curtain between them and discovery. Lights came on, and she felt like a possum in a car's headlights. Instead of going back to the room he'd originally unlocked with a legitimate key, Clay silently moved toward the second room he'd paid for and they quickly scampered over to the next balcony.

Just as her feet landed, the glass door of the balcony they'd just left opened. Clay spun around, gave the man his back and pulled her against his chest so that she remained completely hidden.

"Darling." Clay's voice carried on the night air. "Are you sorry we eloped?"

Eloped? Despite her heart beating so hard that blood rushed to her ears, she immediately caught on. "Daddy has no right to tell me what to do. I'm a grown woman."

Clay chuckled. "You certainly are. And I know just how to make you happy."

"Yes, you do. Take me inside, honey," she cooed. "Let's make a baby."

Somehow Clay picked another lock and ushered her inside while keeping his body between her and the man next door so he couldn't catch a glimpse of her. Once there, she flung herself onto the bed and was about to speak, but Clay placed a gentle hand over her mouth and shook his head, a warning not to talk. He pointed to the microphone, and she realized those men had access to the same equipment as Clay had.

"How about a shower?" he asked.

"Oh, sweetie. I love doing it in the water." She followed him into the bathroom and watched him turn on the water, knowing it would disguise their whispers.

Then he leaned forward and spoke into her ear, "We can talk now if you keep your voice down."

"Do you think they have my brother's stuff with them?"

"Probably."

"What's going to happen when they find out that tape is missing?"

"I'm hoping they think they dropped it. But I didn't get a chance to relock the last door before we fled. The agent may remember that after he finds out the tape is missing."

"Now what?"

"We need to get out of here. But let's wait until our neighbor goes to sleep."

Right now that shower looked mighty good to Melinda. She wished for her bag that they'd left in the other room so she could change into clean clothes. But there was no point in letting all that hot water go to waste.

"Would you mind if I used the shower?"

Clay gestured that it was all hers and left, then closed the door behind him. She started to lock the door, then hesitated. He might need to tell her something, and she had no need to lock him out. She hadn't known Clay long, but she already knew he wasn't a peeping Tom.

But suddenly, she wondered if removing her clothes was a good idea. Especially when she recalled her neighbor. However, Clay would stand guard, and he wouldn't have told her to go ahead if he thought the situation still dangerous.

Deciding to take a quick shower, grateful for the soap and shampoo provided by the hotel, Melinda removed her clothes and stepped under the water. It felt great to wash away the day's salt, sand and tension.

She'd meant to be quick, but she lingered, unable to resist thoroughly washing the debris from her hair that she'd acquired earlier in the day when Clay had tackled her on the beach. She even used the body lotion the hotel provided before slipping back into her clothes.

Leaving the shower water running so she and Clay could exchange a few words if necessary, she stepped into the room. Once glance told her she was alone.

Clay was gone.

He'd abandoned her with the bad guys right next door. She wanted to scream his name. Instead, biting on her lip to keep silent and heart rising up into her throat, Melinda fled back into the bathroom and locked the door.

Chapter Six

Clay quietly closed the door behind him, surprised by the dark hotel room. When he'd left Melinda in the shower, the lights had still been shining brightly.

While he could hear the water still running in the shower, and Melinda might still be there, he sensed another presence in the room. A short, sharp intake of breath, the softest rustle of clothing, a tiny flicker of movement in the darkness. Moving slowly and silently, he eased Melinda's bag to the floor and drew his gun.

Leaving her alone, even for just a few minutes, had been a mistake—one he wouldn't make again. She couldn't have had time to fall asleep on the bed, and he prayed that she'd remained safe in the bathroom, that he wouldn't stumble over her body on the floor.

He shifted his back around the corner to face the beds and balcony. In the darkness that cloaked the room due to the knockout shades and drawn curtains, he couldn't see his hands holding his gun. Couldn't see the furniture. Or his foe. He navigated the room from sheer memory, like a blind man.

Slow and easy.

Another fragile rustle of clothing made him turn his attention from the bed to the curtains. Had the indistinct sound come from that direction? Although he'd locked the balcony door behind him, he knew how easily the lock could be picked. It would take only a moment for an intruder to hit the light switch and draw the curtains shut.

Without knowing exactly where Melinda was, his options were limited. Leaving, he didn't consider. Flipping on the light and ordering the intruder to come out had a certain appeal. But if Melinda was still in the shower, she could walk out into bullets flying.

And there was always the chance the intruder had grabbed Melinda and was holding her a silent captive with a knife to her throat behind the curtain. The mental image had him breaking into a sweat. As much as he longed to attack blindly, he wouldn't risk hurting anyone until he knew their identity.

Which left him back at square one. Prowling at a snail's pace, silently merging with the darkness, making the blackness his friend. Muscles tensed and ready for battle, he used his memory of the room's layout, combined with his outstretched foot feeling his way to advance cautiously through the darkness.

Then his foot tangled in the curtain, warning his opponent. Out of the darkness and through the curtain something glanced off his head and hit the floor. Wood cracked. Clay shifted and raised an arm cocked at the elbow to defend himself against a second blow.

Instead, someone barged into him. He grabbed a

shoulder, spun his assailant around and flung him onto the bed. He closed the distance, landing on top. Small and wiry, the man fought, kneed and elbowed, but Clay simply used his weight to subdue his foe.

A long wet strand of hair slapped his face. Suddenly an awful, mind-numbing thought occurred to Clay. "Melinda?"

"Clay!"

Confused, he rolled from atop her, found the light switch and flicked it on. "What the hell's going on?"

"It's you!" Melinda blinked at the light and stood, her wet hair a mess, her face so pale it was almost luminous, her entire body trembling.

The realization that she was frightened battled with his desire to step forward and comfort her or turn the television's volume on loud—just in case of microphones next door. Necessity made him choose to turn the television up and then, when he stepped forward to comfort her, Melinda's rigid scowl and dark frown kept him from taking another step. She fisted her hands on her hips, squared her shoulders, and when she lifted her chin, he could see her eyes blazing with fury.

He reholstered his gun and shook his head. "I thought someone had snuck into the room."

"So did I." She tossed her head, flinging her hair out of her eyes. "I came out of the bathroom to find you'd left me alone. I thought the bad guys might have gotten you. My first instinct was to go back inside and shut the door but then I realized I'd only trapped myself."

But she hadn't stayed in the bathroom. Oh, no, not

Melinda. She'd hidden herself and came out fighting like a prizefighter. "Go on."

Her eyes narrowed. "Why did you leave me? Do you know how frightened I was thinking that something had happened to you? Where were you?"

She had been worried about *him?* For a moment he didn't say a word, just stared at her in amazement.

Finally he gathered his wits and glanced at the bag he'd retrieved and left by the door. "I thought you might want a fresh change of clothes after your shower." At his admission, her eyes softened. He shook his head and sagged into a chair as he realized the severity of his mistake. He'd put her in danger and the thought rocked him right down to his core. It was one thing to theorize that he might not be qualified to protect a woman in serious danger, quite another to think his mistake could have cost Melinda her life. She could have been killed. He could have lost her—permanently. The thought ripped his gut. She had come to mean much to him in a very short time. "I should never have left you."

The last anger in her eyes died, and her face softened with understanding. "You could have told me that you intended to leave."

"I'm sorry." He ran a hand through his hair. It was one thing to know he wasn't cut out for this kind of work, it was another to have it proven to him. Hell, he could have accidentally shot her. He might get her killed yet.

He'd seen the forgiveness in her face when he murmured an apology, but he couldn't forgive himself as easily. He had to do a better job of protecting her. He needed to be more responsible, more careful.

Just thinking of all the possibilities, running the scenarios through his head, made him feel worse.

The possibility of never again seeing her toffee eyes shine bright with curiosity or her full lips curve up in a pleased smile set him on edge. A sharp slippery edge where falling could prove fatal to both of them.

"I forced myself to come out of the bathroom. I was too afraid to go out the front door and headed to the balcony. I heard footsteps and doubted I could escape in time."

It had been *his* footsteps that she'd heard. "So you turned out the lights and drew the curtains?"

She stepped over to him, her eyes showing her former confusion. "I didn't know what to do." The confusion cleared as she nailed him with a frown. "Sorry, I could have hurt you."

"I'd deserve it. What did you hit me with?"

"A picture frame. It was the only thing within reach."

He chuckled. "I'm just glad you didn't have a gun."

She leaned closer, close enough for him to smell her clean scent. As she peered at his head, a wet strand of hair curved provocatively down her throat. "That's not funny. I'm glad I didn't hurt you."

He pulled her closer and whispered into her ear. "With all the commotion in here, someone may have called security. Or our friends next door might have gotten curious. We need to go."

"I thought you wanted to wait until they went to sleep?"

"I've changed my mind." Having her almost sitting in his lap while the adrenaline seeped from his bones created an intimacy that he needed to escape. Her fresh scent had him distracted, daydreaming over the possibility of turning back the bed, diving into those clean sheets and discovering if she tasted as good as she looked. He stood and held out his hand to her. "Let's get out of here."

"WHERE ARE WE GOING?" Melinda asked from her seat beside Clay in the car as he pulled out of the hotel parking lot and onto a busy two-lane highway. Amid the traffic, she felt anonymous, safer. Still, she occasionally glanced into the side-view mirror checking for a tail.

He drove smoothly, his long fingers commanding the steering wheel with a strength that reminded her how easily she'd put her trust into those hands as he'd helped her climb from one balcony to the next. Those large hands, with strong, clever fingers made her wonder what else he could do with them. She thought about what it might feel like to have him explore her, wondered if his touch would be fast and feverish or slow and sensual, and realized she had little knowledge to go on. Despite the simmering sexual attraction she had so much trouble ignoring, the man hadn't so much as attempted to make a move on her.

"I'm taking you shopping." All business, Clay merged with the traffic, changing lanes frequently, never letting up on his vigilance.

Shopping? "For a tape recorder?" she guessed, eager to hear the messages left on her answering machine. "You think my brother, Jake, has called?"

"We'll find out soon enough."

Clay swung into a parking lot. At this time of night, the area was still crowded with work-weary mothers, harried fathers and teens just hanging out. He took her hand as they strolled through the crowd, the tape burning in her pocket.

As she and Clay walked into a department store and, under bright lights, toward the office and stationery section, she wondered if the rogue agents had yet discovered that the tape was missing. They strode past clothing, then towels and glassware, finally stopping before several brands of answering machines.

She scanned the various choices, recognizing that none of the machines matched hers. "Do you think those men have already listened to my messages?"

"Yes." Clay pulled a box off the shelf. "This one looks as if she'll work."

"So if my brother did call—"

Clay opened the box and pressed a button; the tape slot opened. "Let's not jump to conclusions."

She placed the tape in his hand and he popped it into the slot. "It fits?"

"Yeah. Now, all we need is a little privacy and some electricity." He paid for their purchase and held the box under his arm.

"Let's hope they didn't erase the tape," she muttered, the last of the adrenaline from their escapade at the hotel wearing off and leaving her with a heavy fatigue that made walking an effort.

They retraced their steps to the car. Wearily, she forced one foot in front of the other, the very long, very complicated day suddenly catching up with her. Tapped out, emotionally and physically, her body demanded rest from her exhausting day. She fought to keep her eyes open once inside the car, but she lost the battle and fell into a deep sleep.

She slept dreamlessly and didn't waken until Clay shook her. She opened her eyes, still slightly groggy, her lids fighting and winning their battle to stay open. A glance at the car's clock told her she'd slept for at least an hour. Looking out the window, she didn't recognize her surroundings on a dark street lit by one bright streetlamp on the corner.

The car sat parked in front of a beach bungalow, within a block of the ocean, she guessed from the distant sound of the waves and the salty tang of the breeze. The simple, weathered gray house with charcoal trim boasted a comfortable-looking front porch with cream wicker furniture, a worn welcome mat and yesterday's newspaper.

Clay grabbed their bags, and they walked from the shell driveway along a stepping-stone path to the front door. She stumbled, and he grabbed her elbow to steady her. His touch on her arm felt natural, protective, and yet set up a little hum in her heart. When she suddenly realized they were about to spend the night together, her breath hitched. "Where are we?"

"It's a beach rental. I've arranged to spend a few nights here through a real estate agency." Clay reached under the mat, removed a key, unlocked the front door and flipped on the lights.

They stepped onto a polished oak floor softened with throw rugs. Beachlike and practical, the main room had cheery bright blue-and-white-striped cushions on the sofas, which matched soft curtains that framed screened windows. A tiny but useful kitchen led to a dining nook. The bathroom, located centrally, was convenient to the open areas as well as the bedroom.

Melinda ducked inside. One bedroom. One double bed with a patchwork quilt and lots of pillows did nothing to make her nerves settle. She returned to the living area to find Clay removing the tape recorder from the box, plugging the cord into a socket and popping the tape into the machine. The idea of him listening to her personal messages didn't make her as uncomfortable as the knowing look in his eyes when he saw the flush on her face.

Mentioning the limited accommodations seemed petty. Yet ignoring them had consequences that loomed too large for her to ignore. A conversation to deal with the practicality of sleeping arrangements could be delayed for several more minutes. First, she needed to hear her messages.

She took a seat on the sofa, flipped off her shoes and tucked her feet under her. She appreciated that he'd waited for her to make herself comfortable before hitting the play button.

The tape ran silently for thirty seconds or so, and her former doubts blossomed into full-grown disappointment. "They erased the tape. Or nothing was on it."

Had all that climbing up and down balconies been for nothing?

Clay pressed stop, then rewind. "Hold on a sec. Maybe we started in the wrong place."

Again, he pressed play.

"It's Sheila, hon. Can you come by and see me later?"

"That's Sheila Hammerstein, my next-door neighbor," she explained. The seventy-five-year-old lady was as spry as a teenager but couldn't see well enough to drive. Melinda usually took her shopping once a week and looked in on her every other day or so.

"Matt Rosen here. I need to cancel my Friday appointment, sorry."

His message needed no explanation. The out-of-shape business executive usually needed her services after he spent a day on the golf course.

"Hey, girl. Ladies' night out at TJ's Friday. Eight o'clock. Be there." Melinda grinned at her friend Charlene's brief and cheery message, which helped cut the tension arcing through her.

She didn't know what she'd been expecting—a sinister message or maybe a threat. Instead, her messages reminded her how much her life had changed in less than twenty-four hours. Yesterday, she'd been an average working adult whose largest problem was saving enough money to open her own business. Today, she'd had her life threatened and was being hunted by the CIA. It made her realize how much she had taken for granted. She liked her life, her friends, her job, her home. And all that had been taken away from her with one malevolent slap of fate.

"Ms. Murphy." A deep voice that Melinda didn't recognize spoke huskily over the tape. "I'd like to talk to you. Please call me back at your convenience." The man left his name, Sam Bronson, and a local phone number.

Melinda creased her forehead wondering if he was

a client, a salesperson or even anyone she knew. While his message sounded mysterious, it also sounded normal.

Clay hit the stop button. "You don't recognize his voice?"

She shook her head, puzzled. "I still don't remember much of my morning." While she yearned to reclaim her memories of those last lost hours, she had much to be grateful for, since the vast majority of her recollections had returned.

Clay hit the play button again. "Yo, Melinda, baby." Brian Kelly, a fellow windsailer and a chiropractic physician who often sent business her way, spoke briefly. "I copped a pair of tickets to Dixie Chicks for Saturday night in Orlando. Wanna be my date, sweetheart?"

Clay slanted a glance at her, and for some reason she didn't understand, she felt obligated to explain. "Brian and I are friends."

"Do all your friends call you sweetheart?"

Before she could reply, Sheila left a second message. "Melinda, how about a pizza bash on the beach tonight? You, me and the guys."

"Her dogs," Melinda explained.

"Don't let me forget to…" They heard a cat meow, several dogs started to bark and she muttered, "Got to go."

Melinda caught Clay's frown and realized he was worried about Sheila. "She's fine. While she may not be able to see two feet in front of her nose, her German shepherd and rottweiler protect her. That chaos you heard was simply the boys chasing Lazy Days, her cat."

Clay popped the tape out of the machine, handed it to her and then took a seat beside her on the sofa. "Sounds as if you have a nice bunch of friends."

Something about the way he said it made her realize he hid a touch of loneliness behind his self-sufficient manner. He'd never mentioned any friends or family, and she'd assumed it was because he worked undercover and sought to protect those close to him from this dangerous assignment. He seemed such a loner, so complete within himself that she had difficulty picturing him with brothers and sisters or even a bunch of friends.

Even sitting beside her on the sofa, he seemed isolated, and she suddenly wanted to break through the barrier he drew around himself. The flicker of vulnerability she saw in his eyes slid under her skin, and she ached to take him into her arms and hold him. Instead, she leaned against him and rested her head on his shoulder.

When he placed one powerful arm gently over her shoulders, she snuggled against his heat. They fit well together, and she took more comfort from his touch than she wanted to admit. Sitting close to him, breathing in his masculine scent, made her feel as if she had come home to a warm cozy place, an exciting place scented with cherry flavors that she could explore at her leisure.

She tipped back her head and, ever so slowly, he turned his head. She admired the hard slant of his jaw, the crisp outline of a muscle in his neck, the angles and planes of his hard face. No smile softened his mouth. And when she raised her eyes to his, she saw a mountain of longing, acres of desire and an ocean of hunger in the intensity of his gaze.

Inch by inch, he lowered his head, giving her plenty of time to avoid his kiss. She waited impatiently, and when he seemed determined to go as slow as humanly possible, she reached up and threaded her fingers into his dark silky hair and yanked him closer, reveling in how easily he allowed her to tug him to her.

She'd never known a nibble could spark such a storm of need. Her insides churned as if buffeted by the wind, her emotions swooping and gliding and spinning in a wild journey of steamy pleasure. Clay's agile mouth slowly explored hers, delving into secret places she'd never known could be so sensitive. Greedy for more of him, she wound her arms around his neck, letting his heat kindle a fire inside her jeans, flames within her heart.

He smelled of leather and salt and pure male heat. He tasted of hot-tempered masculinity and man-fired need. She responded, by giving and by taking, with an urgency that came from a place so deep inside she hadn't known it existed.

Breathless, stunned by her own hunger, she pulled back, knowing her eyes must have shown her astonishment at her reaction to him. Melinda had been kissed before, but she'd never responded with such an overwhelming appetite that she wasn't sure whether to flee, or stay—and feast.

"That was some kiss," Clay said with a huskiness she recognized as desire, his warm breath fanning her ear.

So he had felt it, too. The extraordinary attraction

that had hummed between them all day had escalated into a full-fledged fury that both scared and excited her. Her heart thrummed with the possibilities while her mind kept telling her to back off.

Slow down, girl. Just because every rebel cell in her body wanted to make love to him with a soul-pulling gravity didn't mean she would let herself fall into the trap of wanting a man who would ultimately prove unsuitable.

Clay's workaholic tendencies would keep him away from a wife and kids every bit as much as her traveling-salesman father who had never been home. She didn't want to let this attraction between them go one step further when there was no future for them.

Yet, as Clay dipped his head and trailed his lips from her sensitized earlobe to her quivering neck, she couldn't resist his caress any more than her sails could resist a strong wind on a bright spring day. His ripping urgency swept her along, buffeting her objections, cajoling and teasing her with the exquisite promise of much, much more.

Planting her palms on his shoulders, she pushed herself back. Drawing a ragged breath, she shook her head, willing her good senses to return. But only her physical senses seemed to be firing on all cylinders, as her nose greedily breathed in more of his musky scent, her eyes found him more than attractive and her fingertips ached to explore the hollow beneath his jaw.

"We need to talk," she told him.

He nipped a spot halfway between her shoulder and collarbone.

"You go right ahead." He branded the hollow of her throat with a lick of pure heat.

"We aren't right for one another."

"Mmm."

"I don't know enough about you," she protested, and then sighed in a delightful moan as his lips found an erotic spot along her jaw.

"What do you want to know?" he murmured, leaning back and pulling her with him until she sprawled across his chest, which gave his hands access to her back. He took advantage by rubbing slow, sensual circles on her appreciative muscles with his thumbs.

"I don't even know your favorite color."

His irises were a misty green fog with a hint of sparkling emerald chips as he stared into her eyes. "Toffee or amber."

"Your favorite sport?"

He laced his fingers into her hair and drew her lips next to his. "Wrestling with a beautiful woman."

Her mouth went dry. "Your favorite meal?"

"You."

Chapter Seven

Clay's stomach swooped, reminding him of his first free-fall jump from an airplane in the moments before he pulled open his parachute. He felt the same roaring in his ears, the same spurt of adrenaline, the same kick of his heart against his ribs. Only there would be no soft landing, since Melinda seemed to have cut his legs out from under him.

He'd fallen hard and had yet to regain his equilibrium after her mind-blowing kiss. She'd tasted like saltwater taffy with an invigorating hint of adventure. She'd smelled even better, reminding him of fine cognac and a flickering vanilla candle that put off more heat than he'd ever imagined possible.

Even now, he couldn't resist exploring her smoothly soft and silky skin, taking pleasure as she let out a happy groan as he worked a kink out of her back. With her sprawled across his chest, her breath heating his neck, he felt contradictorily patient and impatient at the same time. He wanted so much more of her, yet didn't want to rush.

He yearned to explore her, wanted to know what she liked, how to please her. But she made it difficult to think as she raised her head and left a nipping trail of tantalizingly tiny bites along the curve of his shoulder.

His hand slid to her waist, dipped under her shirt to explore her narrow waist, her delicately curved and muscular back. Tossing her hair out of her face, she peered up at him, placed a palm flat on his shoulder and pulled back.

Her eyes smoldered with passion and a tinge of caution. "I'm not ready to do more."

"You will be." He removed his hands from her back and laced them behind his head.

She arched an eyebrow, took a deep breath. "You sound very sure of yourself, mister."

"I'm sure of what we're feeling. You can't deny you want me."

"I want lots of things."

"And you should have them all." He remained on his back, keeping his hands behind his head, vowing not to gather her close again if she wasn't ready, but admiring how good she looked with her pupils dilated with desire, her lips swollen from his kisses.

Her bottom lip quivered just a tad and then steel straightened her backbone. "Life's not that simple."

"It can be, if you let it."

She sat next to him, her hip next to his. "This is too soon for me."

"What's really wrong?"

At his question, she looked down and twisted her fingers together. "I don't want to like you."

She didn't? At first he wanted to demand why not. But then he realized exactly what her words and actions revealed. She may not want to like him—but she did. She might not want to kiss him—but she had. She might not want a physical relationship, but her flushed face and ragged breathing told him she'd responded to him in spite of her wishes. He couldn't contain a satisfied grin.

"You're laughing at me," she accused him, but he didn't feel the least bit guilty.

"Maybe." He turned on his side to give her more room on the sofa, bent one elbow and propped his head in his palm.

She dusted off her hands and stood, her indignation making her raise her chin a notch. She looked so proper, keeping her resentment in check, that he couldn't resist reaching out, braceleting her wrist and tugging her back.

"If you dare say I look good when I'm mad, I swear I'll slap you," she threatened.

"You always look good."

In the flash of a heartbeat, her anger disappeared and she chuckled, shaking her head at him. "Did anyone ever tell you that you're impossible?"

He failed to contain a grin. "I can't help it if I'm charming."

"Charming?" She picked up a pillow and flung it at him.

He ducked and tugged her closer until she leaned back against him. When she settled comfortably, he tried to keep the need from his tone. "So just how long do you figure you can keep fighting your feelings for me?"

"Until you give up?"

"I'm a very persistent man."

"I noticed."

"It took me six years to crack a Russian code."

"Is that how long you've been with the CIA?"

"Actually, I first worked on the code while I was in military intelligence." *Worked* wasn't exactly the right word. He'd become obsessed with his job, coming home to shower and for a change of clothes. He'd finally thought his wife had stopped worrying over his workaholic tendencies, when instead he'd learned that she'd left him.

"And before that?"

"The usual. College."

"Let me guess. You just studied in college and had no time for fun?"

"I did minor in music."

"That's how you relaxed?"

"Mathematical logic, linguistics and music are made up of patterns that fascinate me."

"Most people study music because they enjoy listening to it."

He shrugged. "When I listen, the notes form four-dimensional models in my mind."

"Four dimensions?"

"Length, width, depth and their passage through time."

She pulled away from him and he let her go. "Well, Dr. Einstein, it's way past my bedtime. I'm going to turn in."

He knew she wasn't ready to make love, but he couldn't resist teasing her, just to watch her face change expressions. "We should sleep together."

At his suggestion, she froze, then sputtered sarcastically. "You're so romantic."

"That's me. Clay Rogan at your service, ma'am."

He stood and made a pompous little bow. "It's the poet in me that's trying to come out."

She laughed and shook her head, her hair spilling over her look of exasperation. "What am I going to do with you?"

He held his arms wide. "How about a hug?"

She moved toward him without hesitation, and he cradled her against him, her head tucked under his chin, her chest and hips pressed to him. She felt right. And while he wanted to make love to her, he wanted her to want him even more.

"We're adults. We can share the bed without making love," he murmured into her hair.

She leaned back and studiously looked at him. "You mean that, don't you?"

"Unless you intend to attack me like a savage, I suppose I'll be safe enough."

She chuckled again. "All right. I promise not to take advantage of you." She glanced over her shoulder at the furniture. "Besides, the sofa is way too short."

So was the bed, but he wasn't about to point that out. Not when she'd consented to spend the night under the same blanket. He let her use the bathroom first, then showered and shaved.

When he returned, she was wearing a long cotton nightshirt and had scooted over to her side of the bed so far she looked like a light breeze would blow her off. He took a seat on his side and realized she was as tense as a virgin on her wedding night.

Didn't she know him well enough by now to realize he would never push her to do more than she wanted? He wasn't accustomed to coaxing unwilling women into bed. In fact, he rarely found the woman unwilling, so he found her inherent distrust of him almost insulting.

"You don't snore, do you?" he teased.

"How would I know?" she muttered, giving him her back.

She really needed to loosen up. He couldn't fall asleep unless she relaxed.

"How about a massage?" he asked.

She turned over and let loose a huff of air. "I charge fifty bucks an hour and only work between the hours of ten and six."

"I meant, how about I give you a massage? And it's free."

"Nothing's free." She lifted her head to look at him. "And I'm sorry. I shouldn't have… Men often get the wrong idea about what I do for a living."

"I understand." He leaned over and placed his fingers along her shoulders on either side of her neck and began to knead her tight muscles. "If I mention I work for the agency, people expect James Bond."

"I'll just bet the ladies all want *The Spy Who Loved Me*." She kept her tone light, but he could hear giant question marks behind her sarcasm.

"There hasn't been a woman in my life since my divorce."

"I believe you. But how many have been in your bed?"

"I'm not a monk."

"And I had no right to ask that question. I'm sorry. It's just that…"

"What?"

"You're going...we're going too fast. I'm not the kind of woman—"

"Who makes love on the first date." He finished the sentence for her. "I know that. It's okay. Now, how about that massage?"

MELINDA KNEW SHE would never fall asleep while sharing the same bed with Clay. She remained on her stomach and didn't feel at all uncomfortable when he straddled her hips. His large fingers lifted her hair off her neck and cool air on bare flesh shot a soft tingle down her spine.

She'd given thousands of massages and there had been nothing sexual about them. As a professional, she loosened tight muscles, flushed fluid from swollen joints, working deeply or lightly depending on client preferences.

Melinda never massaged the men she dated, preferring to keep her work professional, her dates personal. She didn't believe in mixing her work life with her social life. Her dates either accepted her take on things or moved on. None of them, however, had ever suggested giving *her* a massage.

None of them had ever kissed her the way Clay had kissed her, either. She still felt all warm and prickly from the shock he'd given her nervous system. One kiss shouldn't have that much power. One kiss shouldn't have that kind of megawatt voltage. One kiss shouldn't have made her wonder where Clay Rogan had been all her life.

Dazed and turned on by his kiss, she'd almost been ready to make love to him. What the hell had he done to her? She wasn't inexperienced. She didn't believe in chemistry so strong it produced spontaneous combustion, yet when he'd kissed her, she'd almost gone up in flames. Shocked by her own behavior, she'd barely said no in time.

She'd thought a massage would relax her. Although Clay was not a professional therapist, his strong hands seemed to find every tense spot. Slowly and methodically, he worked her shoulders and neck, kneading the soft tissue, finding pressure points and releasing tight knots.

He was good. Unconventional. Expert enough to make a living with his hands.

"Where did you learn?" she asked, her tone muffled a bit by the mattress.

"China. Thailand. India."

"During your stint in the military?"

"I could answer that question, but then I'd have to kill you," he teased. "The information's still classified."

Just when he'd had her convinced he sat safely behind a desk for a living, he threw new tidbits at her. She recalled riding with him on that motorcycle clutching black leather, climbing over balconies, and now with his references to his adventurous past, she realized there was more to him than sitting behind a computer and breaking codes.

That was why she'd picked up danger signals from the start. She might not have had all her memories but there had been nothing wrong with her instincts. Clay Rogan was very likely one of those men about whom women had romantic fantasies. A dangerous rogue. A spy. He'd swooped into her life like a night shadow and then would leave for his next assignment on the wind.

She refused to fall for that kind of man. Yet, as his fingers worked out a spasm near her spine, she let out a soft moan of pure pleasure. "You feel wonderful."

"Glad to be of service."

His words evoked images of what other kinds of services he might provide. She couldn't help wondering whether, if she removed his shirt, she'd find toned muscles and tanned skin. Would he have chest hair? Or be smooth-skinned?

With his powerful shoulders, which tapered to a flat stomach and slender hips, she suspected he would move like a dream. But none of his physical attributes could possibly explain how he affected her libido. His hands on her back made her more aware of a man than she'd ever been. Her pulse beat at time and a half. Her veins sang with their own rhythm. And her heart felt full.

Damn him. She didn't want to like him. Didn't want to respond to him like some lovesick teenager who couldn't control her raging hormones. Yet, she had to grit her teeth to muffle another groan of pleasure as he caressed and stroked the knots in her lower back.

It would be so easy to turn over and draw her hands through his marvelous hair and taste his mouth once more. She could tug him down on top of her, and they could both lose themselves in the passion flashing like heat lightning between them.

But what about afterward? Way after he finished this mission and moved on to the next?

If she gave in to desire now, how would she feel later, after he left her? And even if they tried to make a go of a long-distance relationship, the odds would be against them. Better not to know how he would feel inside her. Better not to reach for the stars when she couldn't always look up and have them within easy sight.

Coward.

She didn't turn over, and if protecting herself made her a coward, then so be it. She may have lost part of her memory. She may have lost a good day's work and a few clients. She might have lost the papers her brother, Jake, had sent her, but she refused to lose her heart to an adventurer.

Melinda believed absolutely that she could chose whether or not to fall in love. Love was a rational decision made upon the basis of concrete things. Things like working in the same town, living in the same part of the country.

She didn't want a fling. Or a short affair. She wanted forever, and if she saw no possibility of forever with a man—then there was no way she would let herself fall in love—even if her veins hummed and her heart overflowed.

The fact that Clay was a good guy, a hunk with a delicious kiss and a mind she could admire, wouldn't sway her. She was not going to make love to him no matter how much her hormones protested. She could control herself. She always had. She always would.

Nevertheless, she told herself to stay away from his potent kisses. Now that she knew how powerful the attraction between them was, she would avoid personal contact. In fact, she shouldn't even be allowing him to rub her back, but he felt so good...

Without warning, Clay suddenly shifted his weight and shoved her off the bed.

"Hey!"

She landed with a thump on the hard floor. Then he was on top of her before she could protest, knocking air from her lungs, covering her mouth with his hand, protecting her with his large and rock-hard body.

Stunned from the hard landing and the way he'd erupted into violence without warning, she barely comprehended his words. Leaning close, he whispered into her ear, "Someone's in the house."

CLAY HAD REACTED on instinct, rolling to protect Melinda and simultaneously grabbing his gun off the nightstand. Now his thoughts raced at roller-coaster speed. All along he'd believed stealing back the tape had been too easy, and now he knew why. The agents had used the tape from her answering machine as bait, no doubt attaching a microscopic tracking device beneath the stick-on label, hoping Clay and Melinda would lead them to the material Jake had sent. Which meant that the agents had already tracked down every lead on the tape and found nothing useful, or they wouldn't have given it up.

The agents must believe Melinda still had the information they needed. Yet, why would they think Melinda and he would try for the tape if they possessed Jake's envelope? And if the agents believed that Melinda didn't have the package her brother had sent, why wouldn't they wait and track them, hoping he and Melinda would lead them to it?

Something just didn't make sense. There could have been a breakdown in communications among the enemy. Someone could be disobeying orders. Or the enemy factions could be fighting among themselves. He suspected a payoff, a double cross or a triple agent's handiwork.

Either way, Clay needed to make some fast decisions. If they were flushed out, he had no idea how many men waited outside to shoot them down or take them hostage, a distinctly unpleasant notion. These men had already shown their ruthless tendencies. Just because he and Melinda couldn't give them the location of the package they wanted wouldn't stop the men from trying to extract that information in extremely unpleasant ways.

Listening intently, he picked up two distinct sets of footsteps, one in the kitchen, the other approaching the bedroom.

Rising soundlessly to his feet, he moved to the open side of the door. By not hiding behind the door, he chose to go for the element of surprise, although he was leaving himself exposed. The problem would be that not only must he take out his opponent on the first strike, he needed to do so in complete silence or his foe would warn his coconspirator.

Clay prayed Melinda wouldn't move or make a sound behind the bed where she remained hidden. As the footsteps closed in, he tensed, knowing he would probably get only one chance. He had to be accurate, deadly if necessary.

Sensing his opponent more than seeing him, Clay

kept his gun ready, hoping he wouldn't have to use it since the noise would alert half the neighborhood.

The intruder, a black mass in the dark room, glided into the bedroom with the stealth of a dark warrior.

Wait.

Wait.

Not yet.

Now.

Using his gun like a club, Clay slammed the weapon onto the back of the man's skull. Ready to strike another blow or catch the slumping body, Clay felt relief as the man collapsed into his arms.

Melinda rolled out from behind the bed and grabbed the man's feet. Together they dumped him on the bed.

"Is he de—"

Clay placed his hand over her mouth. Apparently she hadn't heard the second man's approach. There was no time to talk, no time to tell her to hide. The second intruder must have suspected trouble because he was suddenly inside the room.

Clay wasn't positioned properly, his back was still to the door. He spun around and pointed his weapon.

Too late.

"Drop the weapon, or the girl dies," ordered an unaccented voice.

It was too dark to see Melinda. His second opponent had to be wearing infrared goggles.

Clay tossed his gun to the floor and waited for a better opportunity to strike.

"Kick the weapon to me."

"Where?" Clay asked, stalling for time as he

backed away from the door toward the nightstand and the lamp sitting on it.

He reached out and found the cord, snapped on the light. Bright lights would temporarily blind anyone wearing night goggles.

The man cursed and fired his gun wildly, spraying the room with a burst of bullets. Clay dived for the man's feet, taking him down in a tackle any NFL linebacker would be proud of. What he didn't count on was a counterstrike.

His opponent wasn't carrying a revolver but a semiautomatic weapon. Already out of ammunition, the man used the gun like a fist. Clay took the brunt of the blow on one shoulder, and his entire left side went numb.

With his right hand, he jabbed the man's jaw, but with both men struggling across the floor, his blow lacked power. Another strike to Clay's head from the gun made his ears ring and he realized he'd made a critical mistake.

He should have immediately tried to control the club, not struck a blow with his fist. Grunting, he lunged, narrowly avoiding another nasty blow.

On the floor, trapped between the bed and the wall, he didn't have much maneuvering room.

Melinda's voice suddenly rang out. "Hold it right there or I'll shoot this thing."

His foe struggled harder, then a shot sizzled by them and struck close enough to spray splinters.

"I don't have a clear shot of his head or chest, Clay. Should I shoot him in the balls?" Melinda asked, her voice tight, controlled and trembling.

At her question, the man stopped fighting. "Don't shoot me, lady. We only came here to talk."

Clay jerked the man to his feet. In his late fifties, he stood at least six foot four and looked to be in great shape. His snake-cold eyes ignored Clay and focused on Melinda. "This could all be over if you'd just give us the documents."

"Who is *us?*" Clay asked.

The snake-eyed agent shrugged. "People who will let you live if you give us what we want."

Clay backed away from the agent and took the gun from Melinda's shaking hand. "You did good."

She looked sick, pale.

"Are you okay?"

"I will be."

Snake-eyes shook his head. "No, you won't be. Do you think the people I work for are going to give up? You've come across material that isn't meant for your eyes. Give it up and you can walk away."

Clay had to give Melinda credit. She didn't say a word, letting him handle the conversation.

Short of torture and maybe not even then, this hard case wasn't going to talk. He was a pro. He wouldn't carry identification, and as much as Clay wanted to give him over to the authorities, they couldn't afford to hang around and answer questions—because more of his friends might show up. Friends with official badges that might make the police turn Melinda and Clay over to the enemy.

"Pack your stuff," he told Melinda.

"What about them?"

"We'll tie them up."

"We're just going to—"

"Walk away."

Snake-eyes smirked. "Walking won't be good enough. Neither will running. There's no place you can hide from the CIA. Look, why don't we make a deal?"

Chapter Eight

Clay tied the men's wrists and ankles behind them with plastic garbage bag ties Melinda brought him from the kitchen. He worked quickly, with little excess motion, as if he'd done this type of work before.

The agents didn't look comfortable on their stomachs with their arms and legs twisted back, but Melinda didn't have much sympathy for their predicament. She refused to think what would have happened if Clay hadn't heard the men's stealthy approach. She knew if their positions had been reversed, the agents would not have been content to simply tie them up and drive away.

Still, something about seeing the men bound and helpless left her with a numb and hollow feeling. This violent world of cloak-and-dagger secrets was not one she wanted to live in. Unfortunately, she liked the alternative, dying, even less.

She packed hurriedly and in silence, not wanting to give away anything, while Clay checked the premises. He returned, startling her just as she placed their packed bags by the front door. He moved with a stealth that kept surprising her. Light on his feet, graceful, he advanced like a jungle cat on the prowl.

"There's only the two of them," he reported as casually as if he'd just told her he expected rain tomorrow. "No one's outside."

Melinda let out the breath she'd been holding the entire time they'd been apart. If anything happened to Clay, she wouldn't last five minutes in his rough and nasty world. But she hadn't been worried over herself as much as over his safety, and that bothered her, too. When had she grown so attached to him? Was it simply because they'd been thrust into danger together?

Or was it something that might last if they managed to stay alive?

When they left the house, Clay handed her a set of keys. "Why don't you drive the intruders' car and follow me. I cut the bungalow's phone line. No point in leaving them communication or transportation nearby. The more we slow them down, the less likely they'll be to pick up our trail."

They ditched both cars at the first opportunity, and Clay rented them another car using a credit card that couldn't be traced back to him. Once they were again back on the road, she had so many questions she burned to ask him that she didn't know where to begin. But her mouth wouldn't form words. For some reason, she couldn't stop shaking, her teeth chattered, yet she wasn't even cold.

She forced deep meditational breaths in through her nose and let the air out through her mouth. *Think calming thoughts. The danger is over.* Eventually her shivering stopped, but she'd never felt so tired in her life.

"How did they find us?" she asked, weary yet unable to sleep while sitting in the passenger seat.

He pulled the answering machine tape out of his pocket. The label had been peeled off. "They attached a transmitter to the inside of the label."

"They knew we would come for the tape?"

"They've been one step ahead of us."

"But why follow us?"

"They probably thought we had Jake's documents or figured we could be...convinced to lead them to them."

Convinced? He'd probably used a CIA euphemism for torture. Refusing to dwell on the nasty subject, she forced down rising panic.

She leaned her head back and closed her eyes. She might be weary, but her brain was buzzing ahead on full speed. "That means they don't have the documents. But neither do we. So where are they?"

"Maybe when your memory comes back, you'll remember."

How could he be so patient? She wanted to scream. Hit something. Pound on the dash. "So what do we do now?"

"First, you need rest. I want to listen to the tape again and track down every person who called."

"Wouldn't those agents have already done that? And don't you need rest, too?"

"They may have missed something. And I usually get by on three or four hours' sleep."

"I suppose you spend all that extra time working?"

"We could make love, if you'd rather," he teased, his tone light and sexy. "But I'm trying to honor your wishes and go slowly."

His gentle teasing made the past hours less nightmarish, more bearable. Her nerves still twitched spasmodically, less and less frequently as they put more miles between themselves and the rogue agents they'd left behind.

"Clay?"

"Mmm?"

"What are the odds of us making it through this alive?"

"Excellent. They want the documents."

"But they think I have what they want. Suppose they catch up and try to *convince* me to tell them what they want to know?"

"I won't let anything bad happen to you." He reached over, took her hand and squeezed comfortingly. "Your memories will come back."

"Suppose they don't?"

"Worrying can't be good for you. You're exhausted. Sleep." His voice turned low. "Tomorrow, after you wake up, you may remember exactly where you put everything."

He was wrong. They spent the night in a cheesy motel. Jake paid cash. She fell asleep the moment her eyes closed and her head rested on the pillow. She awakened with a kink in her neck and the sun shining through the windows, indicating that she'd slept away half the morning, and without any improvement in her memory.

Usually an early-morning riser who awakened cheerful and ready to go, she felt grumpy and disoriented, and her head ached. While she took a shower, Clay ordered breakfast. She washed down aspirin with lukewarm orange juice and skipped the runny eggs and soggy toast. Clay ate everything, seemingly unmindful of the terrible food.

For a man who'd teased her about making love, he didn't appear to have any trouble ignoring her this morning. Thoroughly engrossed in his work, he stared into the tiny screen of his Palm Pilot until she wanted to kick him just to gain some attention.

His work ethic seemed turned on twenty-four/ seven, and yet, as she watched him frown over his screen, she couldn't keep from thinking how sexy she found all that condensed concentration. She pictured gears turning within gears, his mind a vast expanse of moving parts, electrical wiring with intense energy driving each thought.

Without looking up from the screen, he offered her a stick of cherry gum. After she refused, he unwrapped a piece and popped it into his mouth. "Those guys we tied up last night work for covert operations. Their names are Aleksi Polozkova and Jon Khorkina."

"Polish?"

"Russian."

"How do you know?"

"I speak both languages."

"Really?" She'd never known anyone who spoke more than two languages. Amazed, she got sidetracked.

"I learned Japanese and Chinese from my mother."

He didn't appear to be even partially Oriental and she frowned. "She's of Asian descent?"

"No. My grandfather was an ambassador and she picked up the languages when they lived overseas. My dad was in the military, and he learned Russian and Vietnamese during the war. Like many European children, I grew up familiar with several languages. The German came courtesy of a grandmother on my father's side."

"Wow. You could have worked for the United Nations."

"Since childhood I've picked up Arabic, Hebrew, Cantonese, Farsi, Japanese and Korean. I suspect it was easier for me since I learned several languages as a child."

All those words in his head. Impressed, despite herself, she realized that, if he wanted, he could say *I love you* in a dozen languages. "You could work as a translator for the United Nations, but I meant how do you know those men's names?"

"While you left to get the plastic ties from the kitchen, I took their fingerprints on my Palm Pilot. The results just came back via scrambled satellite X-U-five."

That was a handy device he owned, and she wondered what else it could do. She couldn't help feeling annoyed that he hadn't mentioned any of this to her last night, but contained her feelings. After all, while she'd been getting her beauty sleep, Clay had been working. "Russians work for the CIA?"

"So do Chinese, Iranians, Lebanese and—"

"I get the idea. How does our government know where their loyalties lie?"

"That's always been a problem. Luckily, when most people defect, they see the economic advantages of a democracy. Many of the agency's most loyal people have fled other countries for their lives and are grateful to be here."

"I assume you're checking out those men—Aleksi and Jon."

"Down to their shoe size."

She couldn't imagine the information was as easy to get as punching in a command for a simple download. "Isn't the information classified?"

"Breaking code is very similar to hacking."

Her eyes widened. "You're hacking into the CIA's classified files?"

"You don't want me to answer that question."

He was right. She *didn't* want to know.

Already too many thoughts swirled in her head. Disturbing thoughts. They'd worn gloves when they'd stolen back the tape, but their fingerprints were all over the beach bungalow. Not only did they now have a lead on the rogue agents, but those agents would soon know Clay's identity.

They'd learn Clay worked in the CIA. She looked over at Clay, who appeared as calm as usual. "We've lost a huge advantage, haven't we?"

"What do you mean?" he asked.

"When those men finally free themselves, they'll find your fingerprints and look up your identity the same way you did theirs. They'll learn they're dealing with a professional who could blow their operation."

CLAY KNEW MELINDA believed the stakes had been raised. She was correct to some extent, but not in the way she thought.

"My prints aren't on file with the agency," he explained.

"Why not?"

"I erased them before I took this assignment." He grinned at her and caught a glimpse in the mirror of his white teeth gleaming like a satisfied lion's after a successful kill. Pleased that he'd had the foresight to outwit their foes, he hoped he could keep outthinking them. While he realized he wasn't playing a chess game with the winner thinking ahead a few more moves than his opponent, keeping his emotions in check helped him to keep a clear head.

"You anticipated this kind of trouble?"

He nodded. "My boss expected problems from the start. We thought it best to conceal my true identity. So, for the purposes of this mission, I'm on my own. And we're safer on our own." Much safer since calling for help might alert their foes to their location.

"Easy for you to say," she muttered.

"Look, once we find those documents, we can hide while I break the code."

"Suppose we don't find them? Suppose we never find them?"

She looked so sad he wanted to gather her into his arms and kiss away her fears. "Oh, I have a feeling they'll turn up." He checked his watch, then picked up their bags. "We need to move out."

"I'd like to check on my neighbor, Sheila," Melinda told him on the way to the car. "Sometimes she needs my help, and I'm worried about her."

"We can stop by later. First, I want to visit this Sam Bronson."

"Who?"

"The man who left the mysterious message on your answering machine. While you slept, I found his address. He works nearby."

Melinda frowned as she slipped into the passenger seat. "He said he wanted to talk to me. What's so mysterious about that?"

"Don't you think it odd he didn't leave a message?"

"Not if he was trying to sell something."

"I spoke to him at home this morning, and he didn't seem eager to talk over the phone. He agreed to meet us for lunch."

Clay knew what he was doing, but he could see doubts on Melinda's face. Undoubtedly, she thought he might be reading more into the phone message than it required, but following every lead, no matter how small, was how cases were cracked. Tiny bits of evidence and information often meant little on their own, but when collated, they often formed a pattern.

"Have you found out any more about the two CIA agents?" Melinda asked.

"My search engine's pulled in some data." He turned a corner and checked the rearview mirror, thankful he saw no sign of pursuit. "What's interesting is that my query flagged several cookies."

"Cookies? Remember, I don't talk spy."

"Sorry. Someone tried to trace my request."

She tensed and looked over her shoulder. "So they're on to us?"

"I hope not. I scrambled and digitized and asked the question in Cantonese—so unless these guys are very, very good, we're still safe."

"All right, then. I'm glad you covered your tracks." She sounded pleased and less wary. "So, we can visit Sheila after we talk to Sam Bronson?"

"Going back to your house—"

"To her house," she corrected him.

"—might pick us up another tail."

"She never calls twice. She must need me," Melinda insisted. "She's a spry enough lady, but cataracts cloud her vision."

Clay drove cautiously, hoping the meeting with Sam Bronson would prove helpful. At least Melinda would eat something during lunch. All she'd had for breakfast was a cup of coffee.

He pulled into the restaurant parking lot ten minutes early. He left the engine running while he took out a pair of binoculars and scouted the area. Off the beaten track, the restaurant was the kind that attracted more locals than tourists. They had a take-out service and a drive-thru that did a bustling trade.

Even with the air-conditioning on and the car windows closed, delicious scents wafted through, tickling his nostrils and teasing his stomach. The one-story block-and-glass building sported tinted windows. The sun's angle and the advertised specials painted on the windows made a thorough check of the inside impossible.

Melinda drew a brush through her hair. "Is that homemade pizza I smell?"

"Hungry?"

"I am now." She started to open the door, then hesitated. "What's the plan?"

"I'm not sure. First, we find out why Sam Bronson left the message on your machine."

Sam Bronson turned out to be a fifty-five-year-old executive with a great tan, sun-streaked blond hair and worried green eyes. When he spotted them from a red-leather booth with a matching red-and-white checkered tablecloth, he stood, nervously glancing at the front door. "I'm sorry for making you drive all the way out here, but under the circumstances, I thought staying away from my regular haunts might be best."

Clay let Melinda slide in first, while he took the aisle and faced the door. He had his weapon within easy reach, although he hoped he wouldn't need to use it. Meeting with Bronson was risky. Especially since his foes had listened to the tape and could be watching the man to see if Clay and Melinda would contact him.

Clay peered closely at Sam's shirt and saw no signs of a wire. But he didn't let down his guard.

A pregnant, tired-looking waitress handed them menus. "I'll be back to check on your order in a few minutes. The lunch special is thin-sliced cheese pizza with capers and olives."

"What circumstances? What's the problem?" Melinda asked, setting aside her menu and facing Sam with a worried frown.

Clay needed to keep his mind on business, but he couldn't resist thinking about how different she'd looked after his kiss last night—happy, excited, reck-

less. She'd responded to him just the way he'd
hoped. No, better than he'd hoped.

Now the frown lines between her eyebrows clearly
told him the stress was getting to her. She wouldn't
be human if it didn't, but he still wished things might
have been different. He wished they'd met under normal circumstances, maybe had dinner, then caught a
movie. He could have walked her to her front door,
stolen a few kisses and asked for another date.

Instead, they'd gone from strangers to almost-
lovers in a few very intense hours. They'd packed
more into those hours than some couples did in years.
Oh, he might not know her favorite brand of perfume
or her taste in magazines, but he knew a lot about
her character.

Melinda Murphy faced adversity with courage.
She knew what she wanted out of life and she wasn't
afraid to go after her goals. She would risk what she
had, push past her comfort zone to reach for success.
Nor had she been afraid to pick up a gun and help
him out of a tough situation last night. Yeah, she was
one gutsy lady.

Even now as she sat beside him in the booth, he
felt her tension. She'd crossed one leg over the other,
her free foot tapping. She leaned forward slightly,
her hands tense and twisting in her lap as if she
feared what Sam Bronson would tell them.

Sam sipped his water, seemingly in no hurry.
''Yesterday, two men came to my house and asked
me questions about you.''

''Men from the CIA?'' Clay asked.

''As a matter of fact, yes.'' Bronson swallowed

hard, his eyes darting toward the door as if he expected the men to show at any time.

"What did they want?" Clay asked, keeping his tone even without difficulty. He'd already anticipated that the agency men would have contacted everyone on that tape.

"They didn't come right out and say what they were looking for."

The waitress returned, and they all ordered pizza and soft drinks. Two booths down, a baby cried and her mother handed her a bottle. A lunch crowd slowly filled up the empty tables. The waitress gathered up the menus and departed before Clay spoke again.

"What did the men ask you?"

"How well I knew Ms. Murphy." Sam folded his hands in front of him. "They had an intimidating manner. You know the kind. Swaggering. Arrogant. They spoke with no accents, yet I got the idea English might not be their first language. They told me that my country needed me to tell the truth." He sighed. "I don't fall for that kind of patriotic talk anymore—not after serving in Nam. Oh, I'm patriotic still, I fly Old Glory on the Fourth of July and Veterans Day, but I don't believe everything I'm told, if you know what I mean."

"I understand," Clay said encouragingly. Sam Bronson might be talkative and slow to come to the point, but the man was extremely observant, which might eventually prove helpful.

"But I saw no reason to lie since I had nothing to hide. I told them Ms. Murphy and I had never met." He hesitated. "I don't think they believed me."

"Why not?" Melinda demanded. "You told the truth."

"Those guys wouldn't know the truth if it rose up and knocked out their teeth."

Melinda nodded, no doubt remembering the two men who'd sneaked into the bungalow. Clay had been around such cold and dangerous men for so long, he'd become hardened to their faults. For a moment he wondered what it would be like to sit on a beach and watch the sunset without automatically tracking which spy satellite was overhead.

The waitress delivered their soft drinks, and Melinda took a long drink, her lips pursing as she sipped and swallowed. "So, why *did* you call me?"

"I should have left a message." Sam lifted his hands, palms up, apologetically. "And I could have told you on the phone, but I thought those guys might have tapped my phone or something. I probably made you drive out here for nothing."

"It's okay." Melinda leaned back as the waitress delivered a large, piping-hot, thin-crust pizza with extra cheese.

The waitress served them each a slice and then left them to their meal. Impatient, Clay refrained from pressing the nervous man, but he really wished he'd get to the point.

The pizza, with just the right combination of spicy tomato sauce and cheese, made him realize how rotten his breakfast had been. Melinda sprinkled hot peppers over hers, then tilted back her head and tipped a slice toward her mouth, her eyes sparkling with anticipation. With her perfectly straight teeth, she nibbled, then took a full bite.

"Good?" Sam asked.

"Mmm."

"So why did you call Melinda?" Clay asked.

"She ordered a case of massage oil from me."

"For the new salon." Melinda nodded, but her forehead scrunched in a way Clay now recognized as a frown. "I'm stocking up on supplies, but I ordered through a wholesaler—not through you."

"I work for the wholesaler and wanted to avoid telling the retail company you ordered from that we screwed up, so I called you direct." Sam hesitated. "This is kind of embarrassing, which is why I didn't leave a message. You see, we manufacture massage oil for therapists, but we also have other...brands. Somehow the products on the last two cases in each lot got an extra ingredient. Luckily, yours were the only ones shipped before we caught our mistake."

Clay helped himself to another slice of pizza. "Is the extra ingredient harmful?"

Sam squirmed in his seat. But he looked Clay square in the eyes. "The added ingredient makes the skin hot."

"Hot?" Clay asked, wondering if this mistake could result in a burn.

"The skin gets hot when you apply the oil and then blow on it," Sam elaborated with an apologetic glance at Melinda.

An erotic massage oil? Clay chuckled.

Melinda didn't look amused. "Thank God I didn't get it and use it on a customer. My reputation could have been shredded."

"I'm sorry. It was an honest mistake. I want to

give you a full refund. Plus, I shipped a new case of regular oil—on the house.''

The waitress placed a check on the table, and Sam picked that up, too. ''My treat.''

They polished off the pizza, and Clay realized they'd wasted time on this lead, but it couldn't be helped.

Sam left the waitress a generous tip. ''Oh, one more thing.''

''Yes?'' Melinda asked.

''When you didn't respond to my phone call, I drove by your office. I mean, your house?''

''It's both.''

''I saw this man peeking through the windows. He was up to no good.''

''How do you know?'' Melinda asked.

''He ducked into the bushes when I drove by.''

Clay downed the rest of his drink in one long swallow. ''Can you give us a description?''

''White. Six feet tall. Medium build. He wore an over-large jacket, like he might have been packing.''

''Packing?''

Melinda looked to Clay for an explanation. ''You think he carried a holster and gun beneath the suit?''

''Yes. His only distinguishing feature was a white tuft of hair at his temple. The rest of his hair was black. And he moved fast, his actions deliberate, not scared. Like he's ex-military.''

''Did you notice if he wore gloves?''

Sam shook his head. ''Sorry, I wasn't close enough to tell. You might check with her neighbors. Maybe one of them saw something.''

Chapter Nine

Melinda kept waiting for Clay to make a crack about the mix-up in the massage oil. Instead, he carefully checked the parking lot before allowing her to exit the restaurant behind him. She found his precautionary measures sobering. While he focused on protecting their lives, she was thinking about erotic massage oils.

Still, she'd bet not one in a hundred men would resist making some off-color comment that would automatically make her defenses go up. Clay just seemed to get it—no explanation on her part required. He didn't ask how many of her clients were men or women, young or old. He didn't ask if men ever came on to her while she worked. He didn't ask what they wore during a massage. He had too much self-confidence to feel threatened by her work.

She'd never met a man who simply accepted her and her profession with such aplomb. Or a man as determined to charm her into his bed. The men she dated tended to be patient. Then again, Clay Rogan was not the kind of man she typically dated.

Who was she fooling? She didn't date much.

She'd had a fling or two several years back, but nothing serious. Nothing that revved her blood and made her so aware of a man's masculinity. Ignoring Clay's six and a half feet of raw sexuality was like trying to crawl out of her own skin. It couldn't be done.

But it was his superior intelligence that she found so seductive. The man worked as one with his computer. She wouldn't be surprised if he thought at transistor speed or if his superior memory held millions of gigabytes of information. She'd bet he'd played chess before he'd started kindergarten, whizzed through calculus and was one of the CIA's most valuable agents.

And therein lay her problem. A man like him took pleasure in using his abilities to the max, testing himself against the best. He wouldn't be satisfied with less. His workaholic tendencies fit perfectly with his getting by on only a few hours of sleep per night. He was obviously good at a job that didn't leave much spare time for a wife.

She wasn't the kind of woman who would settle for so little. Never would she build her life around a man who put work ahead of family. She recalled all too well how miserable her father had made her mother. The time spent waiting for him to come home, the tearful goodbyes. And the worst part, never knowing when he'd return.

It had been even worse when she was a child with no control over the situation. She'd never known if her father would be home to see her act in the school play or sign her report card or remember to at least phone on her birthday. Melinda's entire early childhood seemed one of waiting for Daddy to come home.

Later her parents had divorced. For a long time she'd believed that if she'd been a better girl, her dad wouldn't have left. As a teen, she could have gotten caught up in that trap of seeking out male attention to make up for the lack at home. Instead, she'd found windsailing and working her way through school to be her salvation.

Melinda wasn't going to make the same mistake her mother had made. No child of hers would endure that kind of lonely childhood. Or go to bed thinking that if she was just good enough, Dad would come home tomorrow. She wasn't going to fall for Clay Rogan. No matter how good a brain he had, or how pleasing she found him, she knew better.

So why did her heart go pitter-patter when he opened her car door for her? Why did she have trouble remembering his unsuitability when he teased her, his dark green eyes glinting like the crest of a wave on a sunny day?

She suddenly wondered what her neighbor Sheila would think of Clay Rogan. Sheila was always trying to fix Melinda up with her eldest grandson, but it was more a running jest between them than a serious plan. However, her elderly neighbor was a good judge of character, and she'd enjoy Sheila's reactions to him.

Clay drove through the darkening skies and an early-afternoon shower that didn't last but a few minutes. Melinda wished the short shower could have lasted a little longer. She liked being enclosed with Clay, hearing the patter of rain on the windows, background noise to the news that Clay always listened to, flipping channels to hear the latest worldwide problems.

When he drove into her neighborhood, she felt as if she'd never left. Children played on their backyard swing sets, rode bikes and played ball. A college student mowed his parents' lawn and waved as they drove by.

When Clay didn't slow, Melinda pointed out her friend's tiny but well-kept house with wildflowers beside a stone walkway and geraniums in the window boxes. "Sheila lives next door to me."

Instead of stepping on the brakes, Clay calmly nodded. "I want to scout out the area before we stop. You see any strangers?"

Just as she was starting to relax, he reminded her—not by his manner, he was calm enough, but by his vigilance—that home wasn't safe. She looked up and down the street, wondering what he saw. Most of the people here were working couples. Several of the moms were fortunate enough to stay home with their kids. The Bradleys down the street had just painted their SUV silver after their teenager's fender bender last month. Carrie's folks had insisted she take a job to pay for the damage, and she was busily sweeping their driveway of pine needles.

"Looks okay to me."

Clay turned around and parked in front of Sheila's house but facing the highway, just in case they needed to make a quick getaway. Melinda realized he made dozens of decisions like that for her safety every hour of the day. While grateful for his security measures and protection, his actions didn't make her feel safe. In fact, they had the opposite effect, reminding her constantly of the possibility of danger.

Drawing a deep breath to help her relax, she let out the air slowly. Across the street, Derrick Johnson peered at her through his window and waved. The African-American dentist was a fellow windsailer and one of her favorite neighbors. A single, handsome forty-five-year-old orchid grower, he always had a smile for her.

Now was no different. He hurried out his front door, a package under his arm. As she and Clay got out of the car, he headed in their direction.

Derrick waved at them, clearly eager to speak to her. Beside her, Clay stiffened, eyeballing the package. "You think that's the papers Jake sent?"

She frowned. "Why would Derrick have them?"

Derrick joined them and shook hands with Clay as she introduced the two men. Derrick held the box under one arm, concealing the label. "This came for you the other morning. I signed for it. Hope that's okay?"

Her hopes rose, but the box didn't look like the envelope she remembered. Maybe she remembered incorrectly. Was this why the CIA agents hadn't found the package? Because Derrick had signed for it?

Clay took the box. "Thanks."

Derrick looked from Clay to her and back. He grinned, winked and gave her a thumbs-up. "You go, girl."

"Thanks for your help, Derrick. I appreciate it." She found his wink odd until after Derrick left and Clay showed her the mailing label.

The package wasn't from Jake. It was from Sam Bronson's company. The package was marked Fragile. And beneath the label someone had handwritten Erotic Oil.

No wonder Derrick had winked at her. After being gone for two nights, she showed up with the hunk of the year in tow, just in time to receive her erotic massage oil. In spite of herself, she chuckled.

"What's funny?" Clay asked, his vigilance never wavering as he perused the street and sidewalk for danger while she placed the box in the car's trunk.

"Derrick's reaction…to you…and the erotic oil. He assumed—"

"He assumed right. I can't wait to put this stuff to the test." Clay peeked over his sunglasses at her, spearing her heart, testing her resolve.

She remembered his strong hands expertly kneading the muscles of her back and shoulders, imagined those hands dipping into the oil, spreading the fluid sensuously over areas he had yet to explore. Heat rose to her face as she tried to will the images away.

She couldn't. And the fact that she couldn't bothered her as much as her physical reactions to this man. It was one thing for her body to admire and lust after a prime male specimen. That was a natural and basic human need that she'd neglected for far too long. But for him to invade her thoughts and daydreams was the ultimate loss of a battle she needed to win with herself.

She'd flat out decided Clay wasn't the right man for her. She would not get involved, no matter how much she longed for more kisses, more caresses.

Sheila poked her head out the door, squinting over her sunglasses. "Melinda, is that you, hon?"

"She has cataracts and doesn't see very well. Try not to scare her," Melinda said softly.

"You think I can turn myself into the incredible shrinking man?"

She tried and failed to keep a straight face. "Try some spy dust. That ought to do the trick," she teased back.

Sheila met them on the front porch of her house. The frail woman wore her dog-walking gear, an oversize T-shirt, tight leggings, walking shoes, a baseball cap, dark glasses to ward off the sun and a cane to fend off attacking muggers—not that she'd ever need one with her German shepherd and rottweiler to protect her, but as she'd often told Melinda, she intended to be prepared.

Melinda hugged Sheila while the dogs sat at her neighbor's hand signal. "I've been worried about you."

"I'm fine."

While Melinda embraced and reassured her neighbor, Sheila peered at Clay. "Introduce me to your *little* friend, dear."

Melinda grinned and did as the feisty old woman asked, enjoying Clay's attempt to keep his face polite, instead of laughing outright.

"So you're the reason she hasn't been home the last two nights—not that I'm counting, mind you." Sheila squeezed Melinda's hand. "It's kind of sudden, but love can come that way. Strikes like lightning or crawls like a snail. Either way, when you know, you know. And, good God, you're glowing—

even I can see that.'' She tugged Melinda toward her front door. "You don't need to be listening to an old woman's prattling. Come in. I'll fix us a little snack.'' She glanced back at Clay as the dogs obediently followed inside. "Make that a big snack.''

Clay shook his head, but Melinda saw the amusement in his eyes. Somehow she'd known he would enjoy Sheila's politically incorrect chatter, but she was glad to have her hunch verified. Their relationship hadn't had time to develop in normal ways. She hadn't met any of Clay's friends or family. Or he hers—until Sheila.

"We just had lunch,'' Melinda told her friend as they entered the overcrowded living room decorated with flowered Victorian wallpaper, a doll collection and pictures of husbands, children and grandchildren. They walked past an upright out-of-tune piano that Sheila's first husband had played, which she still kept for the sentimental value.

While Sheila had a large and extended family, none of them lived nearby. Melinda had taken it upon herself to watch out for her neighbor and had enjoyed their friendship. "I've been a little busy lately, but wanted to stop by and make sure you're okay.''

Sheila took her favorite seat in a lounge chair, the dogs curled up at her feet as she waved her guests to a soft pink couch. She peered through cataracts from Clay to Melinda, her mouth quirking in a pleased smile. "Now I know why you didn't answer my phone calls.''

"We aren't having a romantic tryst,'' Melinda said

firmly, avoiding Clay's eyes. "Someone's after me, and Clay is trying to protect me."

Sheila raised one speculative eyebrow. "That's not romantic?"

Clay chuckled and Melinda wanted to kick him. The last thing she needed was for the two of them to gang up on her. Obviously Sheila thought they'd already slept together, and Clay couldn't have acted prouder.

Ignoring Clay as best she could, Melinda scooped Lazy Days, Sheila's cat, onto her lap. She scratched behind the cat's ears and was rewarded as he purred with contentment.

"So why did you call me?" Melinda asked.

"I called three times. The first time I thought I'd walk on the beach while you sailed."

"Sorry, I didn't get the message in time."

"No problem."

"The second time I called because I was worried about you. But I see you're in good hands."

Clay chuckled again. "Glad you think so."

Melinda ignored the implications of those double entendres. "Why were you worried about me?"

"Well, you were kind of upset."

"I was?"

"I may be old but I'm not senile. You were all upset over that package your brother sent you."

"I don't remember discussing it with you."

"Well, I do." Sheila's tone remained tart but she looked puzzled. "There's nothing wrong with my memory, is there?"

"Of course not." Sheila's sister had Alzheimer's, and as a result, the elderly woman worried unduly about losing her own mental faculties. "I had a car accident," Melinda explained, "and banged my head. I'm the one who can't remember what happened that day."

"Oh, God! Are you all right?"

"I'm fine. I was hoping you might have seen a stranger lurking around my house. A friend said he saw someone."

"Nothing. You know how bad my eyes are. Unless someone is as big as Clay, I'm afraid…"

"Ma'am, you mentioned you called a third time?" Clay reminded her.

"Oh, that was odd. Her machine didn't pick up. I figured the recorder was full." Her last call must have been made after the CIA swiped Melinda's tape. "I just phoned to see if Melinda wanted any of my canned tomatoes. I grow them in the backyard."

Clay kept his tone mild. "Can you tell us why Melinda was upset after receiving her brother's package?"

"She's afraid of having a family. She doesn't like letting people get close to her. I'm surprised she and you… Don't mind me. I'm just an old woman. What do I know?"

"That's all we talked about?" Melinda asked.

"You had a client. You left in a hurry and said we should talk later."

"She didn't say anything else about what was in the papers she received?" Clay pressed gently.

"Learning she has a brother and a sister shocked her. I assured her having siblings can be a wonderful thing. I thought she was calmer when she left, but apparently she still wasn't thinking straight."

She wasn't sure she wanted Clay to hear her conversation with Sheila about having a family. Although she couldn't remember their conversation that morning, she knew Sheila's feelings on the subject quite well.

"Why do you say that?" Melinda asked.

"Well, dear, you rushed off so fast that you left your things behind."

"I did?"

"What things?"

"The items your brother sent you."

CLAY COULDN'T RESTRAIN his grin as Melinda accepted the envelope from her neighbor. He'd never expected the old lady to just hand over the files and photographs, had trouble believing Sheila hadn't already been questioned by the rogue CIA agents.

Before Clay could move on to decoding the documents, he preferred to have all the facts. Although this puzzle was solved, he liked for all the pieces to be filled in.

He turned to Sheila. "Did any government officials question you about Melinda?"

"They did."

"What did you tell them?" Melinda asked, clearly as curious as he was, her hands twisting around themselves in her lap.

Sheila's scrawny chest puffed up with remembered anger and pride. "Those men had no business coming to my home, trying to intimidate me, asking for your personal papers. I pretended to be hard-of-hearing and they left right quick."

"Can you remember exactly what they said?"

Clay asked, trying to figure out whether or not the rogue agents knew what was inside the package.

"'Course I remember."

"Well?" Melinda prodded, unlocking her hands and scratching the cat, clearly taking comfort from his purrs.

Clay wondered how he could get her to pet him like that. He ached for her to turn to him for comfort, but she never did. At first he'd thought she didn't need anyone because she seemed so strong. Then he thought she just didn't want him. But ever since that kiss, he'd known she feared intimacy with him because of the sizzling attraction.

He held on to that thought, telling himself that going slow was good. Letting the heat build to a flame would only work in his favor—if he didn't get scorched. But he couldn't fully contain his impatience. Didn't she yet know that he wouldn't hurt her?

"After the men scared Lazy Days, they said you had come by some old papers that might get you into trouble. That if I knew anything about them and didn't tell, I could get into trouble, too."

"Oh, Sheila." Melinda's eyes brimmed with tears. "You shouldn't have risked—"

"Lazy Days has good instincts. I signaled the dogs to growl and I had my cane."

As he pictured the frail woman shaking her cane at the rogue agents, Clay didn't know whether to smile or frown. If she'd set the dogs on the agents, the men might have pulled their weapons. The courageous woman had gone out of her way to help

Melinda, seemingly never doubting Melinda's innocence.

"Ma'am, we're in your debt." Clay stood, walked over, lifted her wrist and pressed his lips to her thin-boned hand.

"Glad to be of help." Sheila stayed in her chair as if all the excitement had tired her out. "And don't you be worrying. If they come back, I'll tell them you went to Chile."

Melinda hugged Sheila. "Better if you claim that you haven't seen us at all."

"All right then." Sheila cheerfully waved them out the door.

Melinda turned back and looked over her shoulder. "I'll call when I can."

"Don't worry about me. Mr. Finley down the road offered to take me grocery shopping. I think he could use some of my company, don't you?"

"She's already working on husband number three," Melinda told Clay as they stepped outside.

"Nothing wrong with my hearing, girl," Sheila called after them. "I happen to like being married. Sex isn't just for youngsters, you know."

Clay shook his head and restrained a smile at Melinda's blush. He really needed to persuade her into his bed soon to relieve some of the anxiety he saw in her warm topaz eyes. Nor would he mind relieving some of his own sexual frustration.

It was difficult to keep his mind on the case while a part of him remained distracted by Melinda's every look, her every change in tone. He'd tried to remain aloof, but it hadn't worked. He wanted her and knew she wanted him back. They had just come to different resolutions of the same problem.

She thought that maintaining a distance would break the attraction. If she kept at it, the only thing that would break would be him.

Reminding himself to stay alert, he forced his gaze away from Melinda and toward the street. Vulnerable walking to the car, he let Melinda carry the package and kept his own hands free and ready to pull a weapon if necessary. While he didn't think they'd been followed, he couldn't be positive.

Back on the road, Melinda extracted the papers from the envelope and looked through a stack of old pictures. "I'll bet my parents are among these people."

"Maybe." Maybe not. He didn't want to comment or prejudge the material until he had time to analyze it properly. "While I doubt there are any useful fingerprints on these documents because they're copies, it might be better if you didn't handle them until I check."

"My prints are bound to be all over them already."

"Yes, but more handling could smudge something useful."

"Sorry. I can't help being curious."

"We'll get to examine them soon enough," he promised. "But first we need to go somewhere protected. Somewhere private where I know you'll be safe, and I'll be able to work."

Her voice came out tight and nervous. "You don't need me anymore. You have the documents. Why don't you just let me off at the corner and I'll walk home?''

Her question threw him into a spin that made his emotions spiral. Exasperation that she wanted to avoid spending more time with him. Fear that she'd leave herself vulnerable to those agents. Impatience that she didn't recognize that he wouldn't let her escape him.

He forced his tone to remain businesslike and kept driving without giving her an opportunity to get out of the car. "You can't return to your old life just yet. It isn't safe. Those rogue agents will return."

Her words rushed out in frustration. "I can't tell them anything because I don't know anything."

"True. But they don't know that."

Melinda clenched her fists, resting in her lap, so hard that the pink flesh turned pale. "Just how long will it take you to break the code?"

"Why?"

"Because I do want my life back. I have bills to pay."

"I'll see that you're reimbursed for your time."

"It's not just the money..."

Was she finally going to admit she was afraid to be alone with him? Afraid she might act on her feelings.

"If it isn't the money, what is it?"

"My clients will go elsewhere."

He swore under his breath. He supposed he was self-centered to believe her every action and thought revolved around him. She had her own business, plans for her future that didn't include him. He needed to bridge the gap, wanted her to be the one to come to him. But she seemed just as determined to stay away.

Perhaps talking would clear the air.

"I want you, Melinda."

"You'll get over it."

Her words might have been flippant, but every muscle in her body tensed as if for war. Her eyebrows drew together and she refused to look at him, her spine straight and taut.

"There's only one way I want to be over you. Naked. In a nice soft bed, with our clothes strewn across the floor."

"Wish all you want. It's not going to happen."

"Yes, it is. You aren't going to be able to resist me."

"I have news for you…you're very resistible."

"And you're not a very good liar."

She tossed her hair over her shoulder and looked out the passenger window. Her body language couldn't be clearer. She was going to ignore him.

But he had no intention of letting her do so, not after he'd glimpsed the simmering heat that she couldn't disguise in her eyes.

"I'm taking you to a houseboat on the St. John's River. It'll be private and romantic. The boat is fully stocked with food."

"I'm not hungry."

He lowered his voice. "You will be."

"Don't you get it? I don't want you."

"You will," he promised. "You will."

Chapter Ten

They drove the rest of the way in silence. An hour later, Clay pulled off the interstate onto a two-lane highway, then turned again onto a dirt road. Tree branches scraped the car's sides and clasped the metal like tentacles. Grandfather oaks shadowed with Spanish moss dominated the high ground; towering cypress mixed with bay and gum trees ruled the brackish low-lying areas of the swamp.

Melinda tried to relax, but the closer they came to their destination the more antsy she became. The gloomy shadows blocked out the sun, and the confinement of the car made her eager to stretch her legs. At first she blamed her dark mood on her surroundings, then decided it was Clay's fault.

She didn't like his smug confidence that she would fall into his arms the moment he snapped his fingers. He'd find out soon enough that she had no intention of becoming his lover. That he seemed to read her swirling emotions and realized how hard she had to fight her own wants and needs only made her more uneasy about their shared living arrangements.

She felt as if Clay had some kind of emotional

hold over her that she couldn't break. Never before had she been so unsure of herself, as if she'd stepped into free fall with no landing spot in sight. Melinda usually set her mind to something and then went about achieving her goal, step by step. Nothing fancy. Just plain hard work that didn't allow her to veer from her intended course.

Her feelings for Clay were far from straightforward. Sure, she liked him and admired him, but there had to be a promise of a future for her to allow herself to love him. Yet, the man was already taken—married to his work.

She half expected him to make a move on her once they boarded the houseboat. But as she stowed her bag in a large cabin with a closet and dresser that was decorated in soft creams and gleaming golds, he started the motor and cast off, piloting the boat away from the dock and onto the slow-moving river of tan water.

A quick tour of the boat revealed three bedrooms, two bathrooms, a full-size kitchen and a connected living-room area where electronic equipment sprouted from the desktop. Apparently, from the start of his assignment, Clay had planned to come here to decode the material and had his equipment ready.

She wandered past the monitors, computers and keyboards to the stern area, which had a patio table and chairs and was shaded by an upper deck. Two personal watercrafts doubled as dinghies and rested on a lift beside two sturdy life preserver rings.

Stepping out onto the patio, she watched the cypress trees go by. Wildlife teemed in the area. Herons and egrets roosted in the trees and dived after large-mouth bass, swamp jack and water-mouth perch. Overhead, a turkey vulture soared and a flock of wood ibis flitted across the treetops. Turtles sunned peacefully on floating logs. The hammering of wood-peckers on dead trees and the persistent song of a Carolina wren added to the loud guttural notes of Florida cranes and the cries of red-shouldered hawks.

She saw no sign of other human beings and real-ized that he'd taken her to a very isolated part of the state. Florida seemed crowded on the coasts, but the interior was relatively empty, and she imagined the river looked much as it did over two hundred years ago when the Indians used canoes to travel here.

Spying a ladder to the top deck, Melinda climbed to the cabin's roof. From the outside cockpit, Clay piloted the boat with an easy competence that made her wonder if there was anything he couldn't do if he set his mind to it.

She'd half expected him to at least attempt a kiss once they came aboard, but he seemed content to steer the boat. He gestured for her to take a seat, then opened a tiny refrigerator, cleverly hidden beneath a console, which revealed an assortment of drinks.

She bent down to peer inside, preferring to let him concentrate on his steering. Logs floated in the river and overhead branches leaned precariously close to the boat in this narrow part of the waterway.

"What would you like?" she asked him.

"You." He shot her one of those charming grins he seemed to use when he wanted to irritate her most. "But I'll settle for a beer."

She handed him an icy bottle and took a soft drink for herself, afraid that alcohol might lower her resistance to him. God knew, it was low enough already, she didn't need her inhibitions coming down, too.

She popped the top, let the icy liquid cool her parched throat, and played with the condensation forming on the can with her fingertip. Looking over the boat's bow as the hull sliced through the water, she spied several large animals in the river.

"Manatees?"

Clay eased back the throttle, cutting their speed to an idle. "Looks like a full-size calf."

A tail flipped up and the mother nuzzled her baby, urging him alongside. Melinda could see scars along the larger one's back, evidence of past run-ins with boat propellers. The only natural enemy these large, gentle beasts had was man.

With No Wake Zone signs in effect for speedboats, the endangered animals were making a comeback throughout the state. As Melinda watched the mother and baby frolicking in the water, Clay beside her, just as awed as she by nature's display, she realized that she couldn't keep fighting herself. And him.

This man was almost everything she thought she wanted. And when she saw the happy light in his eyes as he watched the manatees frolic, her last wall of resistance fell.

No one was perfect. Least of all...her.

She could no longer deny to herself what he'd seemed to know all along—that she wanted him with a hunger she'd never felt before. She must be crazy out-of-her-mind in lust, because suddenly she didn't care and couldn't remember why they were wrong for one another. Longings too strong to suppress surged to the surface.

Leaning over, she placed one hand on his shoulder and peered down into the water. He wrapped an arm around her waist and tugged her into his lap. "If we head upriver, there's a spring where the herd gathers during the winter. We might find a few more manatees still there."

"Can we swim with them?"

"We can feed them. I have lettuce in the fridge."

She leaned against him and sipped her soft drink, dreamily wondering how long it would take him to kiss her. He didn't, leaving her on the edge, about to dive off a cliff.

Instead, he inched the throttle forward, increasing their pace, and tugged down the brim of his hat to shade his eyes from the setting sun. "I'd like to anchor before dark."

"Anything I can do to help?"

"You know anything about computer equipment?"

"Huh?" Startled, she looked into his eyes to see that he was serious. "I was thinking more along the lines of opening a glass of wine, maybe barbecuing a steak on that grill I saw hanging off the stern."

"Once we find a safe anchorage, I need to work. The galley's stocked. Help yourself."

"What's her name?" she asked him several minutes later as he lovingly uncovered his equipment and plugged in cables, cords and satellite uplinks.

"Whose?"

She'd found a bottle of white wine in the fridge but no fresh meat. There was steak and chicken in the freezer. She took two wineglasses from the cabinet, uncorked the bottle and poured them both a glass. "Your machine's name?"

"Lolita." He shot her a sheepish grin. "How did you know?"

She handed him a glass of wine. He took one sip and carefully set it down on a table so if it slipped, the fluid couldn't possibly damage his equipment.

"I imagine you and Lolita spend more time together than most married couples."

He shrugged. "My work is also my hobby."

His work was his life. While the meat thawed, she sat on the sofa and watched him work. First he booted up his machine, entered a bunch of codes and pressed a thumbprint on the screen before he was cleared to continue.

"Could you hand me your mother's diaries, please?"

She did and watched as page by page he scanned in the entire contents of her mother's hand-written notes. Next he scanned in the photographs and finally the letters. He worked meticulously, methodically, never taking another sip of his wine.

She figured he typed over a hundred words per minute, and she took great pleasure in watching his fingers race over the keys with the control of a concert pianist. His jaw occasionally clenched and the muscles in his neck sometimes tensed, but for the most part he appeared totally relaxed.

And unaware of her. He seemed to concentrate so deeply that she could have set the boat on fire and the smoke would have had to disturb his breathing before he'd have noticed.

After all his talk about sex, she hadn't expected to be ignored and couldn't decide whether to be amused or insulted. When her stomach growled with hunger pangs, she remembered the chicken thawing on the counter.

She found charcoal and lighter fluid by the grill and lit it without difficulty. Returning to the galley required walking past Clay, who didn't look up from the numbers fanning across his monitor. She found fresh lettuce and the makings for a salad, placed two potatoes in the microwave oven and set the timer to start in about twenty minutes, figuring it'd take the chicken thirty minutes longer than that to cook.

A half hour later, she'd set the table, tossed the dressing into the salad and removed the barbecued chicken from the grill. Clay still worked at the computer, seemingly oblivious to her or the scent of grilled meat.

"Clay?" she murmured softly as she poured herself another glass of wine. "Can you take a break to eat?"

"Soon."

Ten minutes later her chicken was getting cold and he was still typing. "Clay?"

"Give me a minute."

"I've given you ten."

"Go ahead and start without me. This is a delicate moment."

Her hunger suddenly disappeared. Here she had been ready to go to bed with him, ignore her principles and just do what she wanted for a change—and he didn't have time to notice.

She cut her chicken into tiny pieces, determined

not to let him upset her. Why should she be so surprised? Had she thought the man would change because he wanted her? Bitterly she realized she should have known better. Clay's personality had been set in stone a long time ago—way before they'd met. He'd admitted that his workaholic tendencies had ruined his first marriage, and he hadn't changed.

As she finished her dinner alone, she realized that someday he might find a woman willing to put up with such neglect, but she didn't happen to be made that way. Any man who needed to work twenty-four/ seven might be a good provider, but he wasn't good husband material, and he certainly wouldn't make a good father.

She left his food on the table, the chicken cooling to room temperature, and thought it was good that she had seen him like this before she'd gotten involved with him. That he hadn't even explained what he was working on made her feel stupid. He'd probably known she couldn't understand his work, but...

What kind of woman would give up without a fight? "Damn it, Clay. You've ignored me long enough."

He kept typing. "Sorry."

"So help me, if you don't turn around and talk to me right now, I'm going to unplug your machine."

"Huh?"

He looked up and shook his head as if to clear it. "Did you say something?"

"If I'd said I wanted to make mad passionate love, you would have missed it."

He stretched and gave her a sideways glance. "So that's what you said?"

Her palm itched to slap him. She'd never had violent tendencies in her life, but he was asking for it. Somehow, she refrained from slapping him. "What I said is that your dinner is cold."

"No problem. I could use a break." He stood, rolled his neck to loosen the kinks and stepped toward the table.

While she found just looking at the cold dinner unappetizing, he cut his chicken and chewed with seeming appreciation. "It's good, thanks. I forget the time and forget to eat when I'm working."

"You're lucky you don't forget to breathe."

She let him eat and appreciated his economy of motion. Ten minutes and he was done, his body refueled.

"This should keep me going past midnight."

She should have known. "You're going back to work?"

He moved from the table back to his computer. "Now that Lolita has all the data, I've got to tell her what to do with it."

She slipped onto his lap, knowing that he could easily see the monitor over her head. "What do you mean?"

"Cryptology is the study of hidden writing. It comes from the Greek word *kryptos,* meaning hidden, and *graphen,* meaning to write."

"I'm with you so far." She leaned back against his chest as his fingers typed and brought images onto the screen. "Are my mother's diaries in code?"

"I don't know yet. A code is a prearranged word, sentence or paragraph replacement system. Unless I can find the system she used, we may never break

the code, if there is one. You wouldn't happen to
know if she spoke any languages besides English?''

"Sorry. I thought the computer would find the pattern.''

"It's complicated. I have no idea which system
she used. Julius Caesar used alphabet substitution
offset by three letters. The word *cat* becomes *gex*.
But since her words read in English, she probably
hid a message within her words. Perhaps we need to
look at only the first letter of the twentieth word on
every page to read her message.''

As he typed and brought up different combina-
tions, she realized that even a simple code could have
thousands of possibilities. They might be looking for
the last letter of the last word on every other page—
or any combination in between. Even with a computer, the process seemed hopeless now that she understood just a smidgen of what he was trying to do.

She leaned back and enjoyed his hard thighs beneath her, using his muscular chest as a backrest.
"So how do you ever break a code?''

"I usually look for patterns. Letters, syllables or
words that repeat or seem awkward. The computer
can call up frequency patterns of letters and words
and compare them to the norm. I look at the rhythm
of words, their placement, their contrast and balance.''

"What's the most difficult code you ever
cracked?'' She didn't mind him working as long as
he kept including her. Besides, sitting on his lap with
his arms wrapped around her lent a certain intimacy
to their conversation and a certain heat as she wrig-
gled on his lap.

"It was a Chinese message. Picture a large curve, then a smaller curve intersecting repeatedly."

She thought back to her high-school biology class. "Like a double helix?"

"More like a large snake and a smaller one crossing over one another's paths. The intersections were the key to breaking the code and allowed the president to sit tight even though the Chinese were amassing troops along their border. We knew it was simply a defense exercise as they claimed, because we'd broken the code."

She wondered how many times he'd stopped their country from going to war. A woman couldn't fight that kind of responsibility, she didn't even want to, so she refused to ask how often his job kept him at work for a night, a week or a month. "My mother must have written those words almost thirty years ago. Won't that make it easier to break?"

"Maybe, but not necessarily. She could have had a key card. Think of a piece of paper with seemingly random holes in it. You place the paper over one page and the letters that show through the holes could reveal the message. Both the sender and the recipient would have the same key paper."

"This seems hopeless."

"Have a little faith, woman. I'm good at what I do."

"So you keep telling me. But I have yet to see any action." She flicked her hair over her shoulder and let it strike him softly across the face, blatantly flirting and knowing for sure she had lost all her marbles.

He leaned forward, nuzzled her neck. Heat blazed

down her spine as he kept typing. So he wanted to play games, did he? She tipped her head back and to the side, capturing his lips, softly, sensuously, nibbling teeny, tiny bites.

Satisfaction filled her as he dropped his hands from the keyboard and wrapped them around her. She twisted in his lap. Kissing him shocked her as heat singed her, blazing pure fire straight into her system.

They'd kissed before. Yet somehow she'd managed to convince herself that the intensity wasn't exactly as hot as she remembered. She'd been wrong. His heat consumed her.

She yanked back as if burned. "This is insane."

"Absolutely crazy," he agreed.

"I don't want to want you," she whispered. "But I can't seem to help myself." And that's when the knowledge struck her like a Mack truck.

She was in love with a capital L. Big time in love. And in big-time trouble. She'd fought against going to bed with this man and lost her heart during the battle.

Damn it! Why did it have to be him? Someone inappropriate. Someone who could so easily ignore her for his work.

Her thoughts flip-flopped, making her dizzy. He'd given her little time to contemplate just how badly she'd fallen. With one hand wrapped in her hair, the other stroking her back, and his wondrously clever mouth on hers, she couldn't draw enough oxygen in her lungs to think straight. Nor could she find the strength or desire to pull away.

Hypnotized by the hunger in his eyes, she drank

of his kiss and wanted so much more that she shook in his arms. For the first time, she knew what it was like to give herself over to the moment.

She could only think about him and how much more she wanted. She couldn't get close enough, tugging his head down, exploring the taste of rich wine on his lips, the scent of masculine heat on his flesh.

"Do you want me?" she asked him with just a hint of tender amusement mixed with genuine need.

"Are you going to make me grovel?"

"Would you?"

"Yes." He lifted her into his arms and carried her up onto the deck. "I want to make love to you under the stars."

"Oh, yes, please."

He set her lightly on her feet, opened a locker and extracted a blanket. He floated it over the deck, and she suddenly wondered what she was doing. Without his touch fogging her thoughts, doubts assailed her. If they made love, how would she feel later after he left her? Did she want to be that vulnerable? But it was too late. She'd already committed her heart.

She would never forgive herself if she turned back now. She wasn't a tease. And she wouldn't deny herself what she wanted more than anything else. She wanted him. His mouth on hers. His hands on her body.

She kicked off her shoes and joined him, standing in the middle of the blanket. Waves lapped against the hull. A gentle breeze blew away mosquitoes. A crescent moon and a cloudless sky lent a hushed, almost reverent atmosphere to their coming together.

She ached to fling herself into his arms, but he held her at arm's length.

"I'm going to undress you."

"Ditto."

"Me first," he insisted, his hands slipping under her shirt and gently tugging it over her head. "It's going to be like unwrapping a present."

"Promise me that you'll tear through the wrapping paper quickly."

"Not a chance. Every moment has to be savored." His warm fingers played with her collarbone, but she didn't want to delay, not with her skin going up in flames at his slightest caress.

She was more than ready for him. "I want you now."

She reached for his shirt and he twisted away.

"So impatient."

"Impatient? I've been waiting all night, but you were too busy to notice."

"I noticed."

"You did?" She would have stepped back in surprise, but his strong palm pressed at the small of her back and kept her rooted before him.

"I couldn't miss your signals," he admitted, unsnapping her slacks and pushing them over her hips. "In fact, I snitched this from the car's trunk."

From his back pocket, he extracted a bottle of erotic massage oil.

She thought he hadn't noticed her earlier, and now, after his admission, she didn't know which was worse—being ignored by him or being put on the back burner. Yet, after sitting on his lap, she clearly knew how badly he wanted her.

He placed the bottle of oil in her palm and closed her fingers around it. "I wanted to let you make up your mind without pressuring you."

"You did?" She stepped out of her slacks and stood before him in her panties and bra, her heart hammering, her palm sweating around the bottle.

"Waiting almost killed me," he admitted softly.

"You could have said something."

"I did."

Heat rushed through her veins and made thinking difficult—no, impossible.

Letting the plastic bottle of oil fall onto her pile of clothes, she stepped closer to him, unfastening her bra and dropping it to the blanket. She didn't need oil to enflame her, not when she already felt like singed toast.

"You're beautiful," he murmured in a husky voice, his gaze taking in her body, clad in nothing more than a triangular scrap of silk.

Fingers trembling, she practically ripped off his shirt, made a mess of unfastening his pants. Somehow the unnecessary clothing fell by the wayside, and they tumbled to the blanket, his arms around her, his chest supporting her.

"Do you like being on top?" he asked, drawing her down until their mouths fused and she couldn't answer.

Except in her heart, which cried out more loudly than she'd have thought possible. Consumed by heat, carried away in a back draft of fire, she reached out to this man on a level profoundly elemental.

Every caress spread the heat, each touch carried her into a blue-white flame of desire. When she finally gathered enough control to slip him inside her, she felt full everywhere, between her thighs, in the bottom of her heart and in the core of her soul.

Then she rocked over him, taking him, urging him on, drawing him with her. Her hips gyrated and a soft moan came from his throat. His moving hips matched hers in a rhythm as elemental as the swamp around them. Her heart cartwheeled, somersaulting her over the edge.

She collapsed onto his chest, her throat raw, her skin slick, her emotions shattered by what they had just shared. Slowly her ragged lungs drew in the needed air.

Seductively, still hard, Clay turned them over until she lay beneath him looking up at the stars. He nibbled her neck while his hands found the erotic oil, which he opened and dribbled over her breasts.

"What are you doing?" she gasped, knowing she still wanted him, but not yet, not this soon, not before her rioting flashes of heat cooled.

His voice, low and husky with promise, set her to trembling. "Now it's my turn."

Chapter Eleven

Clay took a very long turn, several turns, enjoying himself in a way he'd never done before. Exploring the raging inferno between them was like walking blindfolded into a storm with heat lightning crackling all around them, electric, exciting and erotic. Yet the sensual experience was nothing compared to the bombshell of his exploding emotions.

He couldn't come to grips with what was happening between them, wasn't sure he should even try to analyze a process so potent, yet somehow tenuous. Figuring out his feelings was like grasping at the wind.

Melinda brought out in him both a tremendous tenderness and a simultaneous and contrasting feral ferocity that he could barely hold in check. He couldn't seem to get enough of her, losing himself so thoroughly that several times he'd feared he might have been too rough, only to have her urge him on.

He'd fully intended to return to work once she fell asleep on the deck, but for the first time ever, he couldn't bring himself to leave. Not even for work.

He was taking too much pleasure in the way she'd wrung him out and left him satiated, his muscles lax.

Breaking the code could wait. Holding Melinda while she slept, caressing her soft, soft skin was too wonderful to give up for a plastic keyboard and monitor. Her breath fanned his neck as she curled into his heat, one leg thrown over his hip with abandon.

He drew the blanket around them and gazed at the stars. Usually he couldn't wait to leave a woman after making love. Instead, once hadn't been enough. The second time barely took the edge off his hunger.

After the third time, he'd lost count, marveling at how he'd reacted to her giving nature. Melinda didn't know how to hold back. And he'd taken and taken. Even now he had to resist waking her again.

He hadn't wanted a personal relationship between them, had done his damnedest to avoid it. But once he'd realized that the two of them were ready to go up in flames, he'd set his mind on having her. Only now, what the hell was he going to do?

He lived in Virginia, she in Florida. He couldn't move down here and quit his job, not without leaving a giant hole in the agency, not without letting down his country. And she had her heart set on opening her business, had been building her client base for years so she could open and operate in the black. He had no right to ask her to give up her dreams or the brother and sister who she must want to meet.

Besides, she'd made it clear she wanted her man at home at night. He let out a long, low groan. He wasn't the right man for her—except in the blanket.

She stirred softly beside him, nestling her head against his arm like a pillow, her hair's sweet scent teasing his nostrils, taunting him into tasting her lips once again. He dipped his head to wake her slowly, when a loud beeping sound made her spring upright.

"What's wrong?" she asked, listening to the electronic page that was calling him back to work.

"Lolita's broken the code."

"She has? How?"

"One of the parameters I gave her must have fit the…" His lips claimed hers, tasting and taking more than he had a right to.

Melinda pulled back just a few inches. "Aren't you going to shut her off?"

"She'll do that by herself."

"Good." She pulled him back for a kiss, her firm breasts jutting eagerly against his chest and making him groan with yearning.

"But she'll go off again every ten minutes until I…" He reached for his slacks, drew them on carefully over his hips and his semi-arousal. One kiss and she'd had him going again. Another minute and he'd have ignored the page.

Hair rumpled sexily, Melinda stood and pulled on her panties and her shirt. "I'm coming, too. If Lolita is going to interrupt us, the least I can do is find out why."

Clay didn't bother turning on the cabin's lights. The monitor would be bright enough and he didn't need to see the keyboard to type. He took his seat and Melinda slid onto his lap as if he were an easy chair.

Since he could see over her head, and she was slim enough for his arms to fit around her, he didn't think she'd have the ability to distract him. He was wrong.

The memories of what they'd shared earlier, combined with his uncertainty about any future they might have, made his typing sloppy.

Several times he had to move the cursor backward, hit the delete key and retype his search questions.

"What are you doing?" she asked in her half-sleepy voice that he found utterly charming and way too sexy.

"Telling Lolita to go ahead and use the search parameters she's set to read through the entire diary and translate the code."

"What's the key?" Melinda asked.

"Would you believe a giant letter X."

"Huh?"

"If we drew an X across every three pages, the word we want is the one where the two lines cross. Simple. Yet difficult to find. Without a computer, I might never have broken it."

"How did Lolita?"

"Several words in the crosshairs are key words that I programmed her to watch for. She compared their locations and—" he snapped his fingers "—ta-da, a pattern emerged."

Slowly words appeared on the screen. As they started to make a sentence, Clay's excitement grew.

Suspect triple agent Bull Dog in our cell has betrayed us all. Going after proof.

Melinda leaned back and looked up at him. "What's a triple agent?"

"An agent who serves three intelligence services and one who usually withholds significant information from two of those agencies at the instigation of the third service."

"So he's a spy?"

"Worse than a spy. If he works for three different agencies, he can feed inside information from the other two to the third service."

"And the cell is like the group my parents worked in?"

"Yes."

"What kind of name is Bull Dog?"

"A code name." He typed in a request and uploaded it by scrambled Sat-Com link to secret files in the basement of a building in McLean, Virginia.

While he waited for a reply, she asked more questions. "So what was the proof my mother talked about?"

"I don't know."

"What do you mean, you don't know? There has to be more. She said she was going after the proof."

"Maybe she got it. Maybe she died trying. We may never know."

"That's...that's unacceptable."

"Ah, so you don't like dangling ends any more than I do."

"This tells us so little." Frustration welled up her throat and into her tone.

"It's another piece of the puzzle."

A Mail Waiting message blinked on his screen. Clay moved his mouse and called up the message. "Bull Dog has been a code name of three operatives. Information followed. Two of the Bull Dogs belonged to agents who hadn't been born during your mother's time. The third agent's dead. At least the files say he's dead."

Clearly discouraged, she leaned back and slumped. "Now what?"

"You go back to sleep. I'll dig deeper."

MELINDA COULDN'T SLEEP. Not with the early dawn shooting a red glow across the gray mist of the morning sky. Instead of tossing and turning, she figured she might as well make breakfast.

She took out the fixings for an omelette—tomatoes, onions, green pepper and ham—then sliced and chopped and recalled how utterly wonderful Clay had been last night. He'd been the best of lovers, exciting yet tender, considerate and intoxicating. He had intimately explored her body, trying a variety of caresses and sensations until he'd discovered exactly what she liked. In fact, he'd discovered things she hadn't even known would please her.

She turned on the stove burner and melted butter in a pan, then fried up the onions and green peppers. She put coffee on to perk for Clay and fixed a cup of hot chocolate for herself, wishing she knew what to do about her mixed feelings about Clay.

He seemed able to shut her out totally as he focused on his work. And yet…last night when she thought he was ignoring her, he had simply been waiting for her to come to him.

She glanced over at him now. Bare-chested, he looked like a warrior doing battle with his computer. Those brawny shoulders had pillowed her head, his powerful arms had lifted her easily more times than she could count. Had he put what they'd shared last night into a corner of his mind? Or was he a jumpy mass of frazzled nerve endings, too?

After setting the table, she broke eggs into a bowl and stirred vigorously. Were all his thoughts for Lolita right now? She hated to think he could shut her out so completely after the wonderful night they'd shared. But she didn't want to ask and have her suspicions confirmed.

"That smells wonderful," Clay told her. She was so surprised to hear him speak, she almost jumped out of her skin at the sound of his voice.

"Think you can tear yourself away from Lolita long enough to eat while the food's still hot?"

"Just call me and I'll be there."

How the man could type at such a speed, and still talk and jest, was really incredible. As a warm glow spread through her, she realized that he hadn't shut her out after all—if she didn't mind sharing him with a machine.

Still, she found herself humming as she poured the eggs into a pan. This respite from danger had left her relaxed and happy for the first time in days. She could get used to making love with Clay throughout the night, waking at dawn and watching the sun rise.

"Let's eat outside on the deck." Was the man a mind reader? He came up behind her, wrapped his arms around her waist and kissed her neck. "Have I told you lately how gorgeous you look?"

"Not since last night. But I haven't even combed my hair," she protested, although she couldn't resist feeling well pleased by his compliment.

They ate breakfast on the stern deck and watched the sun come up over the swamp. Slashes of pink and purple splashed the sky, awakening day creatures and sending night creatures to their haunts. Early-morning fog was burnt off the water as the sun rose.

They ate in awed silence, saying nothing until the sun broke across the sky. The temperature warmed quickly and she soaked up the rays.

Food finished, Clay leaned back, a satisfied gleam in his eyes. "I suppose I should get back to work."

She placed his plate on top of hers, put the silverware on top, ready to carry the dishes back to the galley. Clay placed a hand over her wrist.

Her pulse jumped, and he must have noted her response since an eyebrow raised. "Stay a moment."

"Sure." She kept her tone easy but felt anything but. Just looking into his verdant-green eyes made her want him again. She wondered what he had done to her to turn her into a sex maniac. Or such a pathetic case that she couldn't get her mind off him.

She already knew the real reason—she loved the man. She would never have responded to him physically without all her emotions in full gear. She just didn't know how to handle herself. The feelings were too new, too raw for her to want to make any decisions. It was easier to drift, live in this moment and not think too much about their future.

"What's the next step? Have you found any other references to Bull Dog?"

"Lolita's still searching, but I'm not hopeful."

"Why not?"

"This mole is buried deep. He's had almost three decades to move up within the agency and destroy any incriminating evidence from his past. He's smart, powerful and he has a huge head start."

"So now what do we do?"

"Send a signal to the agency's D.O." At her puzzled look, he explained, "The head honcho."

"Can the signal be traced?"

He took her hand and squeezed. "Unfortunately there's always a possibility of an interception and trace. But it'll be in code and very brief. Before I send the message to Lionel Tower, I want us packed, docked and ready to drive."

"What about your equipment?"

"What about it?"

"You scanned my mother's diaries onto the hard drive, and Lolita has the code. Can her memory be read by anyone else?"

"Before we go, I'll destroy the drive."

Melinda regretted they would have to leave the swamp so soon. She'd wanted to spend more time with Clay, would have enjoyed swimming with the manatees. But now that Clay had broken the code, he had no excuse to delay.

They motored back to where they'd left the car and transferred their belongings into the trunk. Clay wiped Lolita's memory and transmitted his information to the D.O.

Minutes later, they drove back down the dirt road, retracing their route. Clay used the wipers to remove a day's grit and dust from the windshield, his face a dark frown as he drove and simultaneously scowled at his Palm Pilot.

"What's wrong?"

"The D.O. sent orders back. He wants me to bring the diaries to headquarters."

"But they're mine."

"He wants me to bring you with them."

He didn't sound happy. She wasn't so insecure that she thought Clay wanted to be rid of her after making love last night. There had been too much between them. "What's the problem?"

"He thinks you're still in danger."

"And?"

"Your brother, Jake, has fled the country."

"He's still alive then?"

"As far as we know."

"And my sister?"

"A sniper tried to shoot her yesterday. But she's fine. The D.O. thinks your family won't be safe unless we solve this mystery."

"I don't suppose he has any useful suggestions?"

"As a matter of fact, he does. Lionel Tower has contacts throughout the world. We might not find Bull Dog in the agency's records, but if he's a triple agent, maybe another country can figure out his identity."

"That's good, right?" She had to ask the question because Clay sounded tight, edgy.

"If Tower starts asking questions, there's no telling who might shake out of the woodwork. I asked him to wait until I brought you to a safe place, but he reminded me that your brother's and sister's lives are also at stake."

Melinda swallowed hard. She knew about her brother and sister, and except for her short bout with amnesia, had never really forgotten they'd existed. But without faces to put with her knowledge, she tended to forget they were in trouble, too.

She'd never had much family, wasn't accustomed to thinking about others. She'd been too busy surviving. Still, she had to do better. While she still wasn't eager to meet her siblings, she would get over it. She kept telling herself she was reluctant because family entanglements were new to her, and she refused to look any deeper for other reasons.

The day had started with such grand hope and passion. Now the sun burning brightly overhead seemed to mock her. And the trip to headquarters in Virginia seemed as far away as the moon.

"THE FIRST ORDER of business is to make you some fake identification," Clay told her as he drove back onto the highway, leaving the swamp, but not his fond memories of their lovemaking, behind.

"Why?" Melinda asked. "Aren't we driving to Virginia?"

"Too predictable."

"But we don't even know whether anyone traced your call to the D.O." She glanced over her shoulder as if expecting agents to materialize out of thin air behind them.

"It's better to assume they'll find the boat and the equipment."

"They still won't know where we're headed, will they?"

She had a point, but he preferred to err on the safe side. "If they find the boat, they needn't decode, only trace back my call to the D.O. to suspect where we might be heading."

Melinda let out a long, low sigh, then tilted her head back against the seat. "I could never be a spy."

"Why?"

"I like to think about things that are going to happen. You spend so much time thinking about variations and planning for alternatives that probably won't occur."

"We call them scenarios. It's why I'm good at what I do. I think ahead more steps than the next guy."

"And I appreciate your efforts on my behalf. It's just I appreciate your *other* nocturnal efforts a lot more," she teased, but he could hear the strain behind her words.

Was she already regretting their night of lovemaking? Her tone sounded almost bittersweet as if she was speaking about a fond memory that she'd left behind, instead of considering this relationship as the beginning of good things to come.

He tried to keep the conversation light. "I'm glad I pleased you. And it's only going to get better between us."

"You're taking a lot for granted, mister."

"How so?"

"You're assuming there's going to be a next time."

He glanced in her direction. She might be sitting in exactly the same position, but her shoulders hitched in tight, the muscles in her neck strained, her jaw clenched. He probably shouldn't probe, but he hated unsolved puzzles. "Why shouldn't there be a next time?"

"I don't want to discuss this."

"I don't understand."

"Because it was too good between us, all right?" she admitted with a rush that had him pleased, confused and emotionally off balance. "I'm afraid you might become addictive."

"And that would be bad because…?"

She totally ignored his question and changed the subject. "How are we going to get me fake ID?"

He refused to let her get away with such evasions when her answer was so important to him. "Addictive? Are you comparing my lovemaking to something bad—like a drug?"

"I wouldn't need a fake ID unless you intended to take me on a plane. Or out of the country."

If she didn't already know it, he could be much more stubborn than she. "You see our relationship as something bad?"

"We don't have a relationship. There is no relationship."

"Then what am I?"

"An aberration." She threw up her hands in disgust. "Did anyone ever tell you that you are impossible?"

"Not in the last forty-eight hours."

"Or that it's rude to interrogate your date?"

"So we don't have a relationship and what we did last night was a date?"

"Can I borrow your gun?"

"Why?" He glanced into the mirrors, wary of danger, but saw nothing alarming.

"Because I want to shoot you. Throw something at you. Attack you."

He chuckled. "You can attack me later. If you need a weapon, there's always the erotic oil."

"I should know better than to try and win an argument with a man who speaks twelve languages.

But all your fancy wordplay doesn't change my feelings.''

"Which are?"

"My business."

"I want your feelings to be *our* business."

"You know what my daddy used to tell me?"

"What?"

"You can want in one hand and spit in the other. Which one will fill up first?"

He shook his head. "If that's the kind of thing your father used to tell his little girl, I'm glad he wasn't around much. Does that saying mean that you can't have what you want?"

"Maybe."

"And what exactly do you want?"

"Last week I wanted to open my own business with the clientele I've been building. I wanted to spend my free time on Daytona beach windsailing with my friends. You think you can find the right words to tell me that you might fit into my life?"

For once he didn't have an answer. He couldn't give up his work. After completing this assignment, he'd return to work on a dozen critical assignments that demanded his round-the-clock attention. For the first time in years, the idea pained him.

Melinda would be opening her business, sailing through the ocean, living life, and he wouldn't be there with her. He imagined they'd share a few awkward phone calls that would dwindle then disappear over time. This episode would turn into a favorite interlude. He would lose her.

Even if he asked her to move to Virginia, give up her friends and business and the sister and brother she had yet to meet, he wouldn't have much time to spend with her. And he thought too much of her to ask her to give up so much when he could give back so little.

What the hell had he been thinking last night when they'd made wild, uninhibited love? For once he hadn't planned ahead, he'd just gone with the flow. No, not a flow—a raging-hot tide of need that had almost drowned him.

Just thinking how good it had been made him want her all over again.

"Clay?"

Her sharp tone tugged him out of his thoughts, making him think that wasn't the first time that she'd said his name.

"What?"

"At the last exit, a car pulled onto the highway. It changed lanes and passed a few cars, then settled one vehicle behind us. It's probably nothing, but I caught a glimpse of the men. They look familiar."

"Like the two who attacked us at the bungalow?"

She nodded. "I'm not positive, but thought I should mention it."

At least one of them had their mind on business. Their conversation about the future had distracted him from his task. He couldn't, wouldn't, let it happen again.

He stepped on the gas, slowly accelerating until he had to swing into the left lane to pass the semi-truck in front of him. As he veered back into the right lane, he saw a white sedan pass the car that had formerly been behind them.

Coincidence? Maybe. But with the semi-truck between them, now might be the best chance he had to lose the tail.

"Hold on tight."

Chapter Twelve

Clay needed to lose the tail as fast as possible. Pressing the gas pedal to the floor, he pushed the car's acceleration to the maximum. Wind roared against the glass. He passed drivers, one gave him the finger, several swore or honked. Behind him the tailing car speeded, too.

Clay was all too aware how quickly Aleksi Polozkova and Jon Khorkina could call in local law enforcement to help in the pursuit, or even military choppers to track them from overhead. The decisions he made in the next few minutes were critical to evading their pursuers.

He took the first exit off the interstate. "Tighten your seat belt."

Beside him, Melinda didn't say a word. Her face had turned pale, and her eyes looked way too big, but she seemed determined not to distract him for even an instant.

Clay's first objective, to gain enough lead so the chase car couldn't keep them in the direct line of sight, was hampered by a lack of traffic and one straight road with no cross streets. With no choices to make except to keep the gas pedal floored, he continued checking the rearview mirror.

"Are we gaining on them?" Melinda asked.

"I don't think so. You have any idea where we are?" Clay asked, praying the two-laner didn't dwindle to a country road. Not that he'd mind confronting the two goons back there, but he would never forget that his primary objective was to protect Melinda. Finding her mother's documents and bringing them and Melinda to the D.O. hadn't changed his mission. It had simply made it more difficult to accomplish.

"Wouldn't your Palm Pilot have access to maps?" she asked.

"Yes, but we don't have time to stop. There isn't even time for me to take my gaze off the road."

Beside him, she reached into his front shirt pocket and plucked out the gadget. "So give me instructions."

Clay would have grinned if he wasn't so worried. What other woman would ask him to teach her to use the complicated device while he drove over a hundred miles an hour? But there was no good reason why she couldn't pull up the information. "The power button's on the bottom right-hand corner," he began.

She made a few mistakes but actually caught on quickly. Her major problem seemed to be reading the tiny screen while the car jolted and hurled over every bump in the road. "According to the Global Positioning System—"

"The GPS."

"—we're about to connect with a major north-south road. If we go south, then west, we can head for Orlando Airport. But I still don't have the fake ID we'd need to fly.''

"Orlando is the nearest airport and probably too obvious a destination. What's the next closest big city?''

"To the west is Tampa. North is Jacksonville and south is Miami.''

"North of Jacksonville is Atlanta.'' He headed north. "That's what we need...a major metropolis and a gigantic airport.''

"But they're still following us. Why are you showing them which way we intend to go after we lose them?''

"Because they'll assume what you just did. They'll think we're going either west or south.''

"Or maybe they'll know you tried to outsmart them and—this is making my head hurt.''

"Sorry. You did great. Turn off the power, close your eyes and rest.''

"While you drive at breakneck speed? While every breath might be my last? I don't think so.''

"We'll lose them at the next truck stop. We just need to arrive a few minutes ahead of them.''

While the highway didn't have many intersections, he'd noticed that the last few truck stops had been busy. A few hundred in cash should buy them a ride out of state.

Clay figured he had a two-minute lead when he careened around a corner and spun out the tires to a screeching halt. While Melinda grabbed their things from the trunk, including their bags and her mother's files, he found a truck driver heading to his cab.

The man he chose to ask for a ride possessed a

wedding ring, an oversize shirt that was too tight around the belly and well-worn shoes. He had tired eyes, thinning hair and wore a frown. A glance into his truck revealed his license and name, Mike Hubbard, and showed pictures of family tucked around the windshield to keep him company.

"How about a ride?" Clay asked, holding out three hundred dollars.

"Sorry, I don't pick up hitchhikers."

Clay peeled off another seven hundred in crisp bills and added them to his offer. "Please?"

Melinda joined him, wrapping an arm around his waist. "We're trying to get to Atlanta for my sister's wedding and our car isn't going to make it. Sally won't forgive me if I don't show up. I'm her matron of honor."

Clay didn't say a word as she did her best to charm the trucker. She'd slipped into the role of hapless traveler as easily as any actress. He was amazed at how easily she concocted a believable and nonthreatening story.

"Mister, please. We're stuck in the middle of nowhere. It'll take days for a tow truck to even show up, and then they'll probably have to fly in parts from Detroit."

"Okay. Hop in."

Clay tossed their things inside and then boosted Melinda into the cab just moments before their pursuers peeled into the parking lot. He kept his head down and fiddled with his seat belt. Melinda dropped her purse to the floor and didn't pick it up until their truck passed the chase car.

Standard operating procedure would slow the

agents. They'd check out the restaurant and the rest rooms, ask people if they'd seen Melinda and Clay. By then, they'd be fifteen miles away and their pursuers would have no idea which way they'd gone.

The trucker eyed them a little warily as they straightened in their seats. "You people in some kind of trouble?"

"Yeah." At Melinda's admission, Clay's heart started to race. Now was not the time to come clean. "My sister's going to kill us if we don't make Atlanta by six."

Clay contained a chuckle. Mike's shoulders relaxed. "Shouldn't be a problem."

They arrived in Atlanta an hour early. The trucker dropped them off at a bus station, where Clay consulted his Palm Pilot. He still needed some fake ID for Melinda before they risked taking a plane. After hacking into CIA records that he had no business seeing, Clay instructed a cabdriver to take them to an address in one of the seedier parts of town.

Clay tipped the driver. "I'll pay an extra C-note for you to wait a half hour."

"Sorry."

The cab peeled off, leaving them on the sidewalk with their bags. Again Clay preferred to keep his hands free in case he needed to draw a weapon to protect Melinda. "Would you mind carrying the bags?"

"Not as long as you stay close."

He didn't blame her for feeling wary. The dilapidated buildings blocked the sun. The cracked sidewalks stank of urine and stale food. Kids with blaring Walkmans scooted by on skateboards. Winos slept off their drunks in the crabgrass, and a prostitute plied her trade on the street corner where she competed with druggies selling crack.

"Come on." He led her up concrete stairs to a door with two dead bolts and barred windows. "This is the place."

Clay knocked loudly. No one answered.

"Suppose no one's home?" Melinda asked.

He tried to cheer her up. "Hey, you did great with that trucker. That wedding story was terrific spur-of-the-moment thinking."

"I'm scared, Clay."

Before he could respond, the dead bolt clicked. The door opened two inches and a tiny black man with bottle-thick glasses peered through the crack at them.

"We're looking for Inky."

The man's voice came out softly. "What for?"

"If you don't know, then you're not him." Clay turned to go.

"Hey, wait a minute." The chain scratched on the wood as he opened the front door. "I'm supposed to get a phone call first."

"Sorry, we're in a hurry. You open for business or not?"

AN HOUR LATER Melinda possessed three driver's licenses under three different names with her picture as a blonde, a redhead with glasses and a brunette with hair down past her waist. The entire process hadn't taken long thanks to the borrowed wigs, but she noticed that Clay got antsy while the pictures developed and Inky left for five minutes to make a phone call.

While the studio where Inky took the photographs had been immaculate, Melinda couldn't wait to leave the neighborhood. She understood the need for the fake identification, but the illegal transaction made her feel as if she'd stepped into new territory.

Finally, with IDs in hand, they exited onto the sidewalk and walked toward the cab Inky had called for them. The driver was about six feet tall with black hair. He stood unusually straight by the car, his jacket bulky, his eyes hidden behind dark sunglasses.

Beside her, Clay moved in on the driver so fast, she didn't have time to gasp. The driver reached beneath his jacket as if to pull a weapon, but Clay moved faster. Charging the other man, Clay slammed him against the car.

As the taxi driver spun around, Melinda saw a white tuft of hair on his head and it jogged her memory. Where had she seen him before? Or heard about him?

Clay pinned the man over the hood with his body. "Who are you? Who sent you? How did you find us?" He pulled out his gun, cocked the hammer and pressed the muzzle to the man's throat. "Talk."

"I'm a friend of Melinda's mother."

"My mother?"

"Your biological mother."

Melinda peered at the stranger. "You came by my house, didn't you?"

Clay didn't move a muscle. "You know this joker?"

"I think he's the man Sam Bronson told us about.

The ex-military guy with a white tuft of hair, remember?''

The fake taxi driver frowned. ''Who's Sam Bronson?''

Clay shoved the gun tighter into the man's throat. ''I'll ask the questions around here.''

''Let's hope you ask the right ones,'' the man muttered sarcastically, not appearing the least bit frightened. ''Because if you don't, I've wasted the last thirty years.''

Clay shook the man. ''What are you talking about?''

''I'm Herbert Silverberg.''

Herbert watched Melinda, not Clay, as if expecting her to react to his name. When she didn't, he let out a sigh of resignation. He turned his hard eyes to Clay, his stare piercing, judging. ''You bringing her in on orders from the agency?''

''And if I am?'' Clay challenged.

''Then you can't be trusted.''

Clay relieved Herbert of his weapon and released his hold on the man. ''We need to go somewhere private and talk.''

Melinda trusted Clay, but she didn't understand what the hell was going on. This man had come out of nowhere, offered several provocative statements that only made Clay more hostile, but when Herbert claimed he couldn't trust the CIA, Clay turned the man loose.

Clay might have let go of the man, but he wasn't forgetting his basic wariness. ''This joker's getting in the back with me. Melinda, you drive.''

Herbert nodded. ''Key's in the ignition.''

"Inky called you?" Clay asked as they all got into the car.

"I had the word out. Only hoped I'd find you before…"

Melinda pulled out of the parking space and onto the mostly deserted street. "Before what?"

"Before…everyone…else." Herbert looked from Melinda to Clay.

"And why would everyone be after us?" Clay asked mildly.

"For the diary. Have you broken the code, Viper?"

"Viper?" Melinda knew she was way out of her depth. Herbert's quiet tone frightened her in a way she didn't understand. He seemed to have secrets in his soul. Dark secrets.

"It's my nickname," Clay told her without relaxing one iota or even showing a hint of surprise at the man's statement. "But how did you know?"

"I made it my business to know."

"And why is it your business?" Clay asked.

Herbert scratched his chin. "I need a private conversation with the lady."

"Not a chance."

"Look. You can tie my hands to the steering wheel. She can be outside the car. You can hold a weapon on me as long as you're out of hearing range."

Melinda frowned. "I don't understand."

"He doesn't trust me," Clay explained.

Herbert caught Melinda's eye in the rearview mirror. "And neither should you, young lady."

A chill iced straight from her heart to her toes as

if she'd wandered into a nightmare. She recalled choking out seawater on the beach, and a strong stranger, Clay Rogan, telling her he'd saved her life. She still couldn't remember that day. Still had no proof he was who he said. He could have made everything up. Except, if he was a liar and merely after the diaries, he wouldn't have kept her with him after he had broken the code. "Why shouldn't I trust him?"

"You should trust no one."

"Including you?" Clay asked, surprisingly patient with the man, as if he couldn't make up his mind whether he was friend or foe.

"Where do you want me to drive?" Melinda asked.

"Take the interstate north," Clay directed. "Our plans haven't changed."

"How about that private conversation?" Herbert asked again, his voice pleasant, his undertone lined with steel.

Clay didn't sound irritated. "What part of no don't you understand?"

Melinda let out a sigh of frustration. She wanted answers, not more arguments. "Look, if you two are going to get into a testosterone contest, you can both get out and walk. I want to know what's going on."

Now that they were in a better area of town, she pulled over into the parking lot of a twenty-four-hour diner. The pink and green neon light flickered inside the car and cast an eerie glow. "Herbert, I trust Clay Rogan. I can't tell you why, but I have good reasons. Anything you can say to me in private, you can say in front of him."

Herbert didn't back down. "You aren't just betting with your life anymore, now you're betting with mine."

"Clay isn't going to kill me. Or you."

"Lady, he works for the CIA."

"I know," she said softly.

"His mission is to find and decode your mother's diary."

"I know," she said again.

Clay frowned. "The problem is how the hell do you know that?"

"I have my sources."

Clay aimed the gun at Herbert's knee. "The source's name?"

Melinda knew Clay wouldn't follow through on his threat. But she had to admire the older man's courage. He didn't know Clay wouldn't pull the trigger and he didn't flinch.

Stubbornly, Herbert shook his head and rubbed his white tuft of hair. "I won't have another death on my conscience by revealing my sources."

Melinda looked from Clay to Herbert. "Another death?"

"Your mother died in my arms."

Melinda gasped. "You killed her?"

"No, my dear, I loved her." Herbert's voice was low and dry, yet his hurt poured through, leaving her no doubt he spoke the truth. "But I waited too long, and she married your father before I ever spoke up. She adored him. So I loved her from afar. I don't think she ever knew how I felt about her. It was my gift to her—that and trying to see that her murderer receives justice."

"But you still feel responsible for her death?" Melinda said softly from the front seat. "How did she die?"

"We were in the Mideast, in a country which will remain nameless. Our mission was to advise. In truth, we were secretly supplying arms to the democratic rebels who were fighting for their freedom."

"In other words, you were fomenting a revolution." Clay translated the spy talk for her.

"History is written by the victors. If our side had won, they would have been celebrating their Independence Day."

"But you lost?" Clay guessed.

"The Soviets backed the other side. They gave the soldiers more guns, more ammunition and more help."

"And my mother?"

"Couldn't see we were fighting a lost cause. She was determined to stay until the end."

"How did she die?" Melinda asked.

"And why do you have her death on your conscience?" Clay added.

"Are you sure you want to hear the details? They aren't pretty. Your mother…she died…in pain." His voice broke.

"What happened?" Melinda asked, no longer sure if she really wanted to know. At the memories, this hard-bitten man was close to tears. Would the story he was about to tell give her nightmares? But like a driver compelled to look at the accident she passed on a busy highway, she had to know.

Herbert drew himself up straight. "During our work we grew close to people in the resistance. We ate with them, slept with them, knew the names of their children. And when it was time to pull out, your mother couldn't leave them behind.''

''Why not?''

''She knew they would be tortured and killed. So she tried to get them across the border, to freedom. We marched day and night in the dead of winter. Mothers, children, babies pushed to the limits of human endurance.''

''You were caught?'' Clay asked.

''We were betrayed.''

A sick feeling washed over Melinda. She knew there was no happy ending. Her biological mother might have died thirty years ago. She had never even known her, but how could she not be saddened by the story of a courageous woman fighting against terrible odds?

Still, Melinda wondered what kind of mother would risk her own life for others when her death meant leaving her own three children motherless? Was she so swept up in her cause that she hadn't spared a thought for Melinda or her siblings? Just the question made her feel selfish and small, yet since her mother's actions had a direct effect on her own life, she felt entitled to answers.

''Did my mother worry about her own children? And where was my father?''

''Your mother worried about her children every moment of her day and night. That's why she sent your father home—she insisted that at least one of them survive. Sadly he didn't.''

''He died in a car accident when we were children,'' Melinda said.

Clay shook his head. "He was murdered. Afterward, the CIA thought the children might be in danger, so they split up the family. And their tactic worked. You were safe until your brother, Jake, dug into the past and found your mother's old diaries."

"Who betrayed my mother?" Melinda asked Herbert.

"We didn't know for sure."

Clay arched an eyebrow. "We?"

"I'm getting ahead of myself. Let me explain the way it happened." He shifted in his seat, totally ignoring Clay's gun. "Our tiny group of about forty people had almost reached the border. One member of our cell, Lion, claimed he knew a guard he could bribe and went ahead to make arrangements.

"We were hidden in a cave. Yet, two hours later, the guerrillas found us. When they walked straight to us, with no searching, we knew we'd either been sold out or Lion had been captured and tortured."

Herbert sighed and licked his bottom lip. He reached over and patted Melinda's hand as if to give her comfort.

"Your mother and the remnants of our cell could have fled. We were healthy. But she wouldn't leave those less fortunate behind. She refused to flee, using her last bullets to defend the rebels. We lasted about two hours before soldiers shot every man, woman and child in camp. It wasn't a battle. We were never offered terms of surrender. It was a slaughter. And they knew exactly where we were hiding."

"My mother?"

"Took a bullet in the gut when she threw her body over a child to protect her. I took a shot to the shoulder, another grazed my head, rendering me unconscious.'' He raised his hand to the spot where the hair grew in white. ''It's never been the same. I like the reminder.''

''What happened when you woke up?'' Melinda asked.

''The soldiers didn't do a thorough job. I'd like to think they were sickened by what they'd done—may their souls rot in hell. But probably they were simply careless. Several of us were still alive, including your mother. I tried and failed to stem the bleeding. She was in terrible pain, and she begged me to end her life.'' Tears flowed down his cheeks. ''I couldn't do it.''

Melinda realized he regretted his weakness. Yet, how many men could have ended the life of the woman they loved? And wouldn't that merciful act have made him a killer? She wished she could say something to ease his pain, but sometimes no words would do the job.

''We tried to carry your mother out, but she… didn't make it.''

''You said *we* tried to carry her mother out. Who else survived?'' Clay asked.

''Two other members of our cell and your mother were still alive. Me and Barry Lee and Lion, who'd returned from bribing the border guards.''

''You're leaving something out, aren't you?'' Melinda guessed.

''Barry Lee and I went ahead to scout the terrain. Lion stayed with your mother. When we returned, Lion was removing a handkerchief from your mother's mouth. When I asked what he was doing, he said he was simply tidying up her body.''

"But?"

"I always suspected he smothered her."

Melinda gasped. "You aren't sure?"

"Lion had an impeccable reputation. He risked his own life to return and help us escape to freedom. But if I'd been sure he'd killed your mother, I'd have shot the SOB on the spot."

Clay's eyes narrowed. "Doesn't Barry Lee cover the CIA for a southern newspaper? If I remember correctly, he won a Nobel Prize a few years back for—"

"Revealing corruption in the agency's overseas operations."

"What have you been doing since then?" Clay asked Herbert.

"A little of this, a little of that. I've spent thirty years hoping to prove my suspicions."

"You think Lion betrayed the entire group?" Melinda asked.

"Yes. He wasn't dead. He wasn't tortured."

"But you just said he has an impeccable reputation."

"I've never had hard evidence. Before your mother died, she spoke of treason and betrayals, but she was delirious. Much of what she said made no sense. She talked about a picture she had of a spy handing over documents to a Russian. She spoke of her diary and a code. She said she suspected a double agent in our cell, maybe a pair of them. When I asked for names, she muttered instead about her husband and babies. I couldn't accuse anyone with the limited information she gave me. I'd hoped her diaries might tell us the truth.''

Melinda and Clay exchanged a long glance. Finally Clay asked, ''Did the man you called Lion use a code name?''

Herbert nodded. ''As a matter of fact, he did. But what difference does it make?''

Clay demanded, his voice cold, yet excited, ''Tell us the man's code name.''

''Bull Dog.''

The same man her mother named as a traitor in her diary.

Melinda's hopes rose. ''Do you know his real identity?''

Chapter Thirteen

Herbert rubbed his white tuft of hair, his face grim. "Bull Dog was code-named for his round face and hanging jowls. Plus the fact that once he sank his teeth into something, he never let go. While he preferred the name Lion, Bull Dog stuck. His real name is Lionel Tower."

Lionel Tower. His boss's name rocked Clay back in his seat. "The CIA's director of operations? Surely you don't expect me to believe…"

But he did. The revelation explained so much. Right from the beginning of this mission, Clay had had doubts about why he'd been chosen to protect Melinda when the job was far outside his area of expertise. He'd bought Tower's explanation only because of the man's phenomenal reputation.

Tower's men must have tailed him since the start. That's how the two agents had tracked them to the bungalow, known they were coming after the tape in the message machine. Tower had warned them. The agents might have even thought they were on a legitimate mission—not even known they were being used as pawns to cover up their leader's treachery.

No wonder Tower intended to keep the mission so secret. He didn't want a team decoding the documents that he feared would name him as a traitor. For thirty years he'd worked his way up in the government, covering his tracks as only the powerful could do. But for thirty years, his dirty secrets had remained hidden. Now that Jake and Melinda had brought them back into the light, the siblings had the means to destroy a powerful man. But how?

"Who's Lionel Tower?" Melinda asked.

Herbert let out a sigh. "The CIA's director of operations. Only one of the most powerful men in the world."

"If you're trying to scare me, you're doing a good job," Melinda muttered, but she wasn't giving up, and Clay admired her determination.

Herbert's eyes gleamed like those of a hunter on the trail of cornered prey. "He's a traitor, and now we have proof."

The implications shot adrenaline straight into Clay's veins. "Tower can marshal the resources of the entire free world against us."

"Are you saying we can't bring him down with the diary?" Melinda asked. "This man who betrayed my mother and those people can't get away with it."

"Can you imagine the damage he's done to our country over three decades?" Herbert added. "Selling dirty secrets. I wouldn't be surprised if his name is attached to some of the ugliest incidents in the agency's history."

"But what are we going to do about it?" Melinda asked.

"Your mother's diaries name Bull Dog as a triple

agent.'' Clay spoke slowly, thinking through the facts. ''What proof do we have that Bull Dog is Tower—besides Herbert's word?''

Herbert sat back with a satisfied quirk on his lips. ''Barry Lee has documents. Files. He's been researching for a long time. He has proof Bull Dog is Tower. What we needed was proof Tower was the traitor. The diaries will provide that final needed evidence to complete Barry's exposé.''

''Hold on a sec.'' Clay scratched his head. ''You want to print this in—''

''A newspaper.'' Herbert completed his thought for him. ''We can't go to anyone in the Justice Department without fear of a leak. A leak means some agency death squad will hunt us down, and we'll disappear along with the documents.''

Melinda bit her bottom lip. ''But—''

Clay cut Melinda off. ''He's right. Once the news splashes across the pages of a major paper, Tower will no longer be able to hide behind his powerful job. And he won't dare touch us without incriminating himself further.''

Melinda shook her head. ''What about my brother and sister? They have copies of the documents and will become targets.''

Herbert took her hand. ''My dear, they've already become targets. Both are safe. Although their documents have been destroyed—one was dissolved by acid, another took a swim in the intracoastal waterway.''

''Melinda's copy is the only one to survive?''

''I'm afraid so. We should make another copy and mail it to Barry,'' Herbert suggested. ''He's the only one who knows the significance of our find and who has the wherewithal to print it."

Melinda started the car. "What are we waiting for?"

As Melinda drove, Clay kept his gun in hand. While he believed Herbert's story, the tale made him all the more cautious. He would prefer to drop Melinda off somewhere safe, then deliver the documents to the reporter himself. He didn't quite believe that Tower had no idea where they were right now. It would have been too easy for the D.O. to have had an agent plant a bug on Clay's gear, on Herbert, or on their vehicle.

And two minutes after they left Inky's place, the forger had probably sold them out.

Even if the forger hadn't gone straight to the CIA with their location, if Herbert had found them outside Inky's, then Tower could, too. Clay pulled out his phone and dialed Lionel Tower's direct line.

The D.O. answered on the first ring. "Yes."

"We're on the way."

"Good. When can the extraction team meet you?"

"We need to come in our own way. I don't trust your team," Clay stalled. "We'll come to you."

"Where are you?"

"Two hours north of Atlanta," he lied by sixty miles.

"Son, there's no need for prevarication, this line is secure."

"If you say so, sir." The D.O. knew that he'd just lied about his location. Did that mean the man could pinpoint his exact position? And if so how? "There's been some complications."

An edge of annoyance colored Tower's tone. "His name is Herbert. He's a double agent and a thorn in my side for far too long, but he's expendable. Let me send a team to extract you."

Clay played for time, wondering if Herbert had been tailed. "We can't be sure of your team's loyalty."

"I'll have a chopper pick you up." The D.O. reeled off coordinates that would take them an hour to reach and hung up.

Damn. They didn't have much time. When they didn't show at the extraction point, all hell would break loose. Their first matter of business had to be copying and mailing the documents, but if Tower suspected they knew he was the traitor, the D.O. had the power to call a Code Ten to find them. With a Code Ten, Tower could claim that terrorists had sent bombs through the mail. He could close airports. Block the interstates. Bring out the National Guard. Run their pictures on television's national news.

They couldn't just run. They had to run smart. They had to outthink a man who had the power to call in local law enforcement's help, or the military's or the FBI's. In addition, Tower had Clay's description and photograph. He could use the national media to claim that Clay was a wanted man, and then even the average citizen could spot him on the street and turn him in.

What they really needed to do was hide—but hiding wouldn't get the evidence to Barry Lee so he could splash the story across page one of Jacksonville's prizewinning newspaper. One by one, Clay ran scenarios through his mind. One by one he discarded each idea until he settled on their best chance.

"We have to split up."

"Good idea," Herbert agreed.

Melinda didn't look happy. "Why?"

"It's too easy to spot us together."

"But you don't even know for sure whether Tower has any idea of our location."

"If Herbert found us through Inky, then Tower can, too."

Herbert shrugged. "I found Inky in the agency files. I had every forger east of the Mississippi and south of the Mason-Dixon Line being watched. Tower will check the airplane tickets, credit cards, car rentals and bus stations. Public transportation of any kind is out."

Melinda put on her left-turn blinker. "There's a copy shop up ahead. Should I stop?"

"Yes. But only use the self-service machines. Try not to let anyone see what you're copying. And copy only the vital pages. You have five minutes. Three would be better."

"All right then." Melinda parked the car. From her tone, Clay could tell she was nervous. He tried to reassure her. "I'll cover you from out here. Since the storefront is plate glass, I'll have you in sight every minute."

"I suppose I'll be less conspicuous alone," she muttered, gathered the documents and exited the car.

Clay slipped out of the back and motioned Herbert to come with him. As he watched Melinda, Clay spoke to Herbert. "Does anyone know you and Barry still talk?"

"Not unless my phone's tapped, and I check it regularly. Why?"

"Going to Barry is impossible. He has to come to us—which shouldn't be difficult if no one is watching him."

"Good point."

"But will he do it?"

Herbert removed some change from his pocket and headed to the pay phone outside the store. "One way to find out."

Clay listened to Herbert make the call, his gaze on Melinda. She'd taken the news of her mother's death hard but had recovered sufficiently to use the copy machine with efficient and crisp moves that reminded him of her hands on him when they'd made love. It seemed so long ago since they'd had that most personal of connections, yet the memory lingered in his mind, coming back to him at the most inappropriate times.

While he longed for a successful conclusion to this mission, he also dreaded it because he knew they would then go their separate ways. During the short time they'd known one another, he'd come to admire her spunk, her adaptability and her heart.

Which made putting her in danger all the harder. Running from the D.O. wasn't the smartest action they could take. Giving the director of operations the documents and asking him to forget his and Melinda's existence would be safer. It would also be treason. He wouldn't consider betraying his country—not even for Melinda.

"Fire in the hole." Herbert's words broke into Clay's thoughts. Herbert spoke softly into the receiver, giving his old friend the code words that meant he finally had the proof the reporter required to run the story.

Herbert then motioned Clay to the phone. He spoke quickly, knowing that any call from the entire city of Atlanta might be traced if Tower nailed down their location.

"You'll have to come to me," he told the reporter.

"Where?"

"I'll let you know. Start driving north. Give me your cell-phone number." Clay memorized the ten digits automatically. He'd have to risk another thirty-second transmission burst later from a pay phone to set up the meet.

Herbert wiped the phone clean of Clay's prints just as Melinda walked out of the copy shop. She handed Herbert a bag. "This is the critical stuff."

"I'm—"

Clay held up his hand to stop the man from speaking. "Don't tell us where you're going."

"I understand. I'll try and lay a false trail before I disappear. Maybe it will buy us all some time. Good luck, my friends." Herbert waved a short goodbye and walked away from them, merging into the shadows.

"You think we'll ever see him again?" Melinda asked almost wistfully.

If he lives. Clay didn't speak the morbid thought out loud. Instead, he ushered her back to the car. "He's survived by his wits and at the heart of his enemy for three decades. I'm betting he'll make it."

"I'LL DRIVE." Clay took the car keys from her, consulted his Palm Pilot and sped into traffic.

"Are we in a rush?"

"We need to go to ground."

"Where?"

"The best place to hide is often an obvious place, but somewhere Tower's operatives won't think to look."

Melinda fastened her seat belt and tugged the strap tight, her stomach lurching as Clay took a fast corner. She hoped Clay didn't intend to park the car in the woods for the next four hours. "You have somewhere in mind? Like a hotel with clean sheets and hot running water?"

Clay shook his head. "That's too obvious. What about a hunting lodge?"

"Sounds fine to me."

Thirty minutes later, Clay checked them in to a single room at the Southern Gentleman's Hunt Plantation. The reception area reminded her of a ski lodge with its log walls and huge fireplace. A few guests shot pool and one read a newspaper. A large television set in the corner blared but no one paid attention to it.

Clay checked them into a room on the ground floor. While their accommodations weren't luxurious, Clay seemed pleased with the back door that led to a terrace and a star-studded sky. She pulled back the spread and bounced onto the bed. "Now what?"

"We wait for Barry Lee to drive north."

She was way too nervous to eat or nap. She wanted to pace. Instead, she bounced the mattress a little more.

"That's not a trampoline."

"Really? I thought I'd try a triple back flip."

He sat beside her and pulled her into his arms. "I've a better idea."

She slanted him a look that had to reveal how much she wanted him. "Yeah?"

"Kiss me."

"I've been wanting to do just that all day," she admitted as she wrapped her arms around his neck. She knew their time together was short, knew these might be the last private hours they might share. She wanted to make them memorable.

He kissed her upper lip. "You know, once this is over, I'm going to miss you."

She murmured into his neck. "Glad to hear it."

"You want me to be miserable?" he asked.

"I want you to want me."

"Why?"

"So you'll know exactly how I'll feel."

He ran a hand over her hip and lightly tickled her rib. "So misery loves company?"

"No. Melinda loves Clay."

At her simple yet bold declaration, he pulled back and looked into her eyes. She would have given all her savings to know his thoughts, but he kept them shuttered and closed her out while she felt as if she'd just leaped out of a plane without a parachute.

"How do you know it's love?" he asked.

"Because nothing else would feel so good yet hurt so much." She spoke from the heart, her feelings out there for him to trample.

He pulled her close, held her tenderly. "I don't want to lose you, either."

That wasn't exactly *I love you*. And from a man who knew more than a dozen languages, she found his word choice sadly lacking.

She'd expected no more, yet the fear of losing him warred with an empty hollow ball inside her that ached more than she could have imagined. He liked her. Yes. He found her attractive. Yes. And maybe with proper attention, his feelings could bloom into something more.

She hesitated, then went for broke. "You know I could set up a shop in Virginia."

His expression didn't change. His eyes remained hard, his mouth in a tight grim line. "I don't want you to give up your future for me."

He might as well have slapped her. Pain burned through her like acid. He didn't want her.

He didn't want her.

He didn't want her.

Jerking back from his embrace, she stood and paced, refused to reveal the tears that burned her eyes and threatened to escape.

CLAY HADN'T EXPECTED Melinda to offer to give up her dreams of setting up her business in Florida and move to be near him. Although touched by her offer, he knew better than to allow another woman to waste time on him. It wasn't fair to ask her to sacrifice her family and friends when he couldn't spend the time with her that was needed to keep them close.

He'd learned that lesson the hard way. He wouldn't make the same mistake again. And if he felt pain at losing Melinda, he deserved it for allowing his barriers to come down. When she kept her back to him, he recognized that she was hurting too, and he ached to take her into his arms—but he no longer had that right.

He picked up his cell phone. "I need to call the D.O. again or he'll be suspicious."

Melinda didn't answer him. She stared out the window, rocking back and forth, her arms wrapped across her stomach, her hands resting at her waist.

He dialed the necessary number, waited for the phone to trigger two satellite systems, which made the call untraceable, before again ringing Tower's phone.

"Yes?"

"We're on the move."

"Estimated time of arrival?"

"Five hours."

"What? You should have made it to the extraction point by now."

"It's the best I can do."

Clay clicked off the line, hoping he'd bought them some time. Next he phoned Barry, who must have been speeding the entire way up the interstate. He kept the call short and gave the reporter directions to the hunting lodge and their room number.

The next few hours passed in a tense silence. He paced. She flicked through television channels, gave up and spent most of her time staring out the window. "This is the hardest part of any operation—the waiting."

"It seems like each minute takes an hour to pass."

"It'll be over soon."

When he looked up fifteen minutes later, Melinda

still hadn't moved from her position at the window. "You hungry?"

She shook her head.

"I could find you a place to hide until the story hits the newspaper," he suggested gently. "I can meet Barry on my own and arrange for—"

"I'm seeing it through."

"Fine. Whatever you want."

She spun around and planted her fists on her hips. "Whatever I want? You mean whatever I want as long as it's not you."

"I never promised…"

"No, you never promised me anything, so your conscience should be clear."

"What do you want from me?"

"Obviously something you aren't able to give." Her breath hitched and suddenly her mouth parted. Behind her, the window shattered.

"Get down." His order came too late.

Her lips let out a little "oof," and she toppled to the floor.

Oh God! She'd been hit. Shot. Every cell in his body froze as if the air just left his lungs. He couldn't breathe, could barely think.

Heart kicking into high gear, he dived to the floor, rolled and doused the light in one smooth motion. In another instant, he drew his weapon and crawled over to Melinda. He didn't waste time to see if she was alive, he shoved her under the bed, protecting her as best he could, knowing it was too little too late.

Oh God. She was hurt. Lying there bleeding, and he felt as if a part of him had died.

Damn. He'd expected the D.O. to wait. Somehow Tower must have traced the signal back to the lodge. His agents had moved fast and Clay wondered how many foes were out there. Even if there were only a few, more would be coming.

Clay had to go on the offensive fast. As much as he hated to leave Melinda, her best chance of survival was for him to take out her shooter. Easing open the door, he used his elbows to crawl out on his belly, his worry about Melinda so frantic that he barely felt the glass digging into his chest and torso and thighs.

Leaving her behind was the most difficult decision he'd ever made. It was his job to protect her and he was leaving her injured and unarmed. Unconscious. Maybe dead.

He prayed not.

That she'd been shot clawed at him and he had to fight down a howl, had to use every bit of his gigantic intellect to focus on what was ahead of him—not what he'd left back in that room. Sweating, pulse pounding, he crawled ahead by inches into the hallway.

When he reached a corner, he stood and listened for the sound of choppers, sirens, running feet or the unmistakable sound of a weapon being cocked. He heard nothing and realized the gun that had fired at Melinda through the window had had a silencer attached.

A silencer most likely indicated that the attacking force was small and didn't want to draw attention to itself. At the realization, Clay's hopes rose a notch. He ducked into a bisecting hallway, sprinted through a hall, ran outside to the pool area and used the bushes for cover.

He forced his pace to slow, made his way to the parking area and the direction from which the shooter must have positioned himself. The woods were close by. An owl hooted and mosquitoes buzzed.

Slowly his eyes adjusted to the darkness. One road led into the acreage that surrounded the lodge, then it divided, heading toward the stable and the skeet-shooting range.

Clay stared at the woods, waiting for a shadow to move, a piece of metal to glint. Something. Anything that didn't belong, which could give him a hint as to the enemy's location.

Finally, a black silhouette rattled a tree branch. It wasn't much to go on. But Clay didn't need much. Walking lightly, he circumnavigated the parking lot, keeping to the edge of the woods, hoping to take the enemy from behind.

He stepped with care, placing his toe down first, then following up with his heel. He didn't want to warn them by snapping a twig or sending a bird into flight.

Minutes passed and sweat beaded on his face, drizzled into his eyes. There had to be at least two of them. Agents always worked in teams.

He weighed the danger of moving fast against the fear of Melinda's lifeblood spilling out unchecked. He reminded himself that he couldn't help her unless he won this battle.

He stopped, listened above the pounding of his heart. A soft rustle, just the faintest of noises, caused him to adjust his direction slightly. The humid air left his clothing sticking to him, the moonless night made his mission seemingly impossible, so he tried to use his other senses besides sight.

He sniffed, knowing his opponent would know better than to use cologne, but Clay might luck out with a hint of body odor or deodorant. Nothing.

Suddenly, he heard the slap of flesh against flesh, like his foe swatting a mosquito. Clay narrowed his eyes, squinting to see through the darkness, and the outline of a man slowly formed. First the head, then the torso and finally the long legs. The man rested, his back against a tree, his face focused on the room where Melinda waited for Clay to return.

Clay inched behind the man, his need for stealth great. He needed to take out the man without a sound, strike so swiftly that his foe had no time to call out a warning.

Three more steps and he'd be in striking distance.

Two steps.

One.

Clay lunged, using his gun like a baton, swinging it down on the man's skull, taking no satisfaction as metal collided with bone. His enemy dropped silently. Clay moved in to break the fall, lowered the man to the ground.

He straightened, ready to hunt the fallen man's partner with no clue to where he might be.

That's when he heard Melinda scream.

Chapter Fourteen

Her scream froze him straight to the bone. Clay had miscalculated. He'd assumed the shooter's partner was somewhere outside, but Melinda's cry for help told him differently.

Fear pounding up his throat with every lunging footstep, Clay dashed out of the woods, across the parking lot, straight back to their room. Fear for her life dogged his every move. He shouldn't have left her alone, and if she died because of his mistake he would never forgive himself.

There was no time to pick the door lock. No time to run through the hallway and retrace his steps. Without hesitating, Clay took the shortest route to Melinda and barreled straight through the open window. He took the brunt of the landing with his hands and shoulders, made a diving roll onto the mattress and tumbled into struggling bodies, losing his gun in the process.

A powerful elbow rammed his side and knocked the air from his lungs. A meaty fist clipped his jaw, slamming his head back so hard his teeth snapped together. With a roar of pain and anger and fear for

Melinda's safety, Clay ignored the sharp daggers of agony that sliced down his neck.

He couldn't extract his spare weapon in the close quarters, couldn't reach for his gun, needing his hands to ward off a series of blows to his head and shoulders. Besides, shooting in the dark could be dangerous to Melinda. He had no idea where she'd fallen.

He focused on taking down his opponent, using kicks and punches before closing in and setting his hands around the man's neck, choking the air from his lungs.

His opponent kicked out, barely missing his groin. Clay squeezed harder and ducked his head as the struggling man tried to gouge out his eyes. Clay rammed a knee into his foe's stomach and the fight went out of him.

"Clay, is that you?" Melinda asked. He saw her silhouette looming over him about to crash a lamp on his head.

"Yeah, it's me. You can put that lamp down. He won't bother you anymore."

Melinda flicked on the light. The lamp slid from her fingers. Blood ran down her arm and side. "Is he dead?"

"Just unconscious." Clay released his strangle-hold on the man's neck and turned to her. Relieved she was alive, worried about her injury, he blamed himself for leaving her alone. "You were shot. You've lost blood. Sit down and let me—"

The door slammed open. A tall, thin stranger with silver hair pointed a gun at Clay. "Don't move."

Again Clay had miscalculated. He'd thought there

were only two agents outside. This man stood too far away for Clay to lunge at him before he could pull the trigger and too close for him to miss. Now they'd pay for his mistake with their lives. That his life should end didn't bother him as much as the painful thought of Melinda dying due to his mistake. She would never meet her brother and sister, never open her business, never make love to him again.

God, he wanted her. Wanted to hold her and love her and tell her he'd been a fool not to accept her offer to come to Virginia. Now it was too late. He braced for the bullet, sorrow overwhelming him that he'd never told her how he felt. Never told her he loved her more than life itself.

If he could have lunged and taken down the third opponent, he would willingly have given his life for hers. But the man stood too far away. Clay could attack quickly, but not that quickly.

"Lady, are you all right?" the gunman asked. "Maybe you should sit down and let me call an ambulance."

Melinda looked at the stranger holding a gun on Clay with one hand, his laptop computer in the other, and started to laugh. It must be the shock. The loss of blood was making her woozy. Still chuckling, she slid down onto the carpet, her back propped against the wall. "You've got to be the only reporter in the world that thinks the gun is mightier than a story."

Clay's mind had been so full of worry over Melinda, he'd failed to consider all the alternatives. The man was carrying a laptop. He'd invited this man here. He kept his hands raised but smiled grimly. "Barry Lee?"

The reporter nodded. "I heard a woman scream and...old instincts die hard." Sheepishly, Barry put away his gun and held out his hand. "Viper, I presume?"

"Call me Clay." Clay gestured to the documents sitting neatly in a stack on the nightstand while the rest of the room looked as if it had been struck by a tornado. "What you need is over there."

While the reporter perused the documents, Clay sat next to Melinda, pulled her gently onto his lap, and searched her body for an injury.

"Here." She lifted her arm and showed him where the bullet had left a bloody trail along the fleshy part of her skin. The wound looked raw and painful but not life threatening.

"You'll be fine."

She cuddled against him. "It hurts."

"I was so afraid I'd lost you. When the bullet hit, you just collapsed. I thought..."

"Would you have missed me?"

"You have to ask?"

Barry rustled some papers. "I hate to break up this touching scene, but we're not in the clear here. I need complete, concise and factual explanations. And maybe we should do it from someplace safer?"

Clay stood and rubbed his forehead. He wasn't thinking clearly. He tore a spare shirt and made a bandage for Melinda's arm while he tried to concentrate on their next move.

When Melinda spied his back, she gasped. "You're hurt, too."

"It's just slivers of glass." He turned to the reporter. "What's your deadline?"

"Midnight." Barry checked his watch. "My editor went out on a limb to save me page one. Most of the story is written, but I have to confirm the facts before we can put it to bed."

"You probably have a lot of questions. You can ask them as we drive out of here."

Clay didn't bother gathering anything but Melinda, letting the reporter keep the papers. Slowly the trio made their way to the car. "When Tower's men fail to check in, all hell's going to break loose."

Barry nodded. "I've been waiting to write this story for over thirty years. A few CIA agents aren't going to stop me."

Clay helped Melinda into the passenger seat and strapped on her seat belt. "Can you type while I drive?" he asked the reporter.

"Sure. Explain how you broke the code."

Ten minutes later, Barry had the last details of his story ready to transmit to his waiting editor. There was only one problem, a red and blue blinking light and a siren from a Georgia sheriff who had spotted their car and wanted them to pull over.

Melinda looked nervously over her shoulder. "You can't stop."

"Tower will kill the story if we're stopped now," Barry agreed. "You're going to have to outrun them."

MELINDA THOUGHT THEY had a chance of outrunning the cop until she heard a chopper hovering overhead. The helicopter flew in low and shined a spotlight on their racing car.

Clay kept speeding down the highway and spoke

calmly to Barry. "How much more time do you need?"

"The story's done. I need an Internet connection to transmit. And for that we'll have to stop." He peered worriedly out the window. "We're not going to make it, are we?"

Clay handed his specialized cell phone to Barry. "You can plug in to my cell phone. We have satellite uplink to the Net. How long will the transfer take?"

"Thirty seconds. Then I need you to buy me another minute or two while I wipe my hard drive clean."

Clay passed a semi-truck, steering smoothly, seemingly unfazed by the growing number of police cars behind them. "You've got three minutes, maybe four."

Barry connected his laptop to Clay's phone and transmitted the story. He typed quickly and erased the data.

Melinda didn't understand why he was bothering to hide the data when the entire world would soon hear about the front-page story, but didn't ask until he finished his work.

"Why erase the hard drive?"

"It'll make it more difficult for the bad guys to figure out what we did," Barry explained.

Clay clarified. "We have to keep our actions a secret until the newspaper hits the streets."

"That's another two to three hours." Melinda looked over her shoulder. No way could Clay evade the cops for that long. She turned back in her seat and, through the windshield, she saw a blockade up ahead. Fear clutched her stomach in a fierce grip. They were about to be caught.

Clay applied the breaks. "Okay. They'll likely split us up and demand that we talk. Stall. Ask for your attorney. Give them nothing until after 3:00 a.m."

Melinda tried to fight through her growing fear. She'd never been arrested. Her biggest legal trouble had been a speeding ticket. Now she had multi-government agencies after her and no idea how many laws they'd broken. "What about my mother's papers? If they confiscate them, we won't have proof to back up Barry's story."

Barry chuckled. "Yes, we will."

She couldn't believe the reporter could laugh or that Clay could appear so calm when she felt nausea churning up her throat.

Barry patted his laptop case. "I photographed the documents and transmitted the pictures with the story. And Herbert still has his copy."

"It's going to be okay," Clay assured her, then turned to Barry. "I don't suppose you brought any fake identification? It would help if the authorities couldn't figure out your identity right away."

"Wouldn't matter anyway. My fingerprints are on file with the agency."

"Then I think misleading the authorities will be best. Tell them you met us to find out why the CIA is harassing a citizen. Tell them you just started to speak to us. If you can convince them you're working on another story, they might just believe it."

"Don't worry, I'm a writer, I'm good at making up stuff."

While the men spoke about deceiving and stalling, Melinda's pulse raced. Of the three of them, she was the least experienced in this game. She was the weak link.

"I'm afraid I'm going to screw up," she admitted as Clay slowly braked.

He reached for her hand, and she welcomed his heat as he rubbed the cold from her skin. "They can't force you to talk. The only thing you need to do is to ask for your attorney. Remember, you've done nothing wrong."

"Okay."

"And remember this, too."

"What?"

"I love you."

Before she could even react to his astonishing statement, he stopped the car. At least two dozen police cars surrounded them. The chopper kept them in a blinding spotlight, making it difficult for them to see outside the perimeter of vehicles surrounding them.

Over a loudspeaker, they heard a man's voice with a Georgia accent. "Open the doors, come out with your hands up."

Melinda started to comply.

"Wait," Clay told her. "Remember, we're stalling for time. "Move slowly. Make them say everything twice."

Her hands trembled. She thought she might be sick as the red and blue swirling lights made her woozy. How could he think so calmly with guns aimed at them from every direction? She took a deep breath, told herself to believe that they wouldn't shoot first and ask questions later.

"Come out slowly. Hands up."

"Now?" Melinda asked.

"Let me go first." Clay cracked his door, pushed it open farther with his foot and raised both hands above the door so the cops could clearly see that he held no weapons.

"Lie on the ground. Arms above your head."

Clay stood perfectly still, his arms held above his shoulders. "There are two more people in the car. A man and a woman. They will come out one at a time. Don't shoot. We have no intention of resisting."

"Lie on the ground. Arms above your head," the voice from the megaphone repeated.

Clay did as they ordered. He moved slowly, taking at least a full minute to go to the ground.

"Will they handcuff him?" she asked Barry.

"Not until we're all out of the car. They won't approach until they're sure it's safe."

"You in the car. Come out, show us your hands first, then lie on the ground."

"Okay." She took a deep breath. "I'll go next." As per Clay's instructions, she waited for the man with the megaphone to repeat his orders. With excruciating patience, she waited then slowly scooted over to the driver's side and exited the car so she could lie close to Clay.

Numb, shaking, she followed the instructions until she lay flat on the pavement, a few loose stones cutting into her shoulder, but she dared not move to a more comfortable position. As Barry followed her out of the car, she asked Clay, "What happens next?"

"It depends on who has jurisdiction."

"What do you mean?"

"If we're lucky, the local cops will want the collar."

"If we're unlucky?"

"The military or the FBI will take us in for questioning. At worst, they'll take us to the CIA."

Barry lay on the ground next to them. The police, weapons aimed and ready to fire, moved in.

"Clay."

"Yeah?"

"I'm scared."

"Anyone in his right mind would be scared. The trick is to think of something else."

Like what Bull Dog had done to her family. The man had probably given the orders to kill both her parents. The man had covered up his crimes for three decades, and he wasn't going to get away with it any longer. They had him cold. All she had to do was keep quiet for three hours. If she lived that long.

As men roughly cuffed their hands behind their backs and shoved them toward the chopper, her legs proved wobbly. Remembering to use any excuse to stall, she let herself sink to the concrete, made two men carry her to the helicopter with no outside markings to indicate which arm of the government had just taken them prisoner.

Was she about to become one of those people who just disappeared and was never heard from again?

No one said a word during the one-hour helicopter ride. They landed at a small airport and were then

placed in a military aircraft. She overheard the pilot
speaking with ground control and learned they were
headed for Virginia. Was this some kind of covert
operation where Bull Dog himself was going to question them?

She shuddered in terror at the thought of facing
the man who had ordered her parents' deaths, the
man who'd betrayed her country. A man who had
the power of practically the entire government at his
command.

WHEN THEY FINALLY landed in Virginia, Barry, Clay
and Melinda completed their journey by another un-
marked helicopter. Clay estimated that they only had
to refrain from speaking another ten minutes or so
before the newspapers would hit the streets, and it
would be too late for Tower to squelch the story.

However, Clay well knew from his training that
ten minutes of excruciating pain could reduce the
strongest of men to a babbling idiot. They possessed
one advantage. Tower had no idea of when the deadline was. Chances were he wouldn't resort to drastic
measures so quickly because he didn't realize the
deadline was so soon.

He'd probably separate them and leave them in
cells to sweat over the possibilities of torture. And if
they were lucky, by then the deadline would have
passed.

MELINDA DIDN'T KNOW whether to be happy or un-
happy about being locked in a cell by herself. Her
wounded arm throbbed, but the pain had dulled.

Here, at least, she wouldn't have to resist answering questions. No one had said anything to her at all.

Sitting uncomfortably on the cot, she wondered how much time had passed. She began to understand after several minutes how the mind could devise its own tortures. She wanted to talk to Clay. She wanted to know the time. She wanted to know who was holding her captive and what they would do next.

Slightly cold and fighting off the growing panic, she warmed herself with the memory of Clay's declaration of love.

Had he really said those words? Or had she wished for them so hard that in a moment of extreme stress, her mind heard what she wanted it to?

Standing, she paced. Surely fifteen or twenty minutes had passed?

Suddenly, she heard footsteps, and her heart skipped in fear. Would she be able to hold out and follow Clay's instructions? Or worse, had they come to shoot her?

Tense, she turned and saw Clay. She let out a breath of relief as he, not some stranger, walked toward her cell, a grin on his face, the key to her cell in his hands. Had he escaped?

"What happened?"

"CNN got an advance copy of the paper. The news broke an hour ago on every radio station. Tower, Aleksi and Jon Khorkina have been arrested. I'll have to testify in front of a closed congressional hearing."

She sagged with relief. "It's over?"

"Yes." Clay unlocked her cell, took her into his arms and captured her lips. "Life's going to return to normal. The day after tomorrow, you can go back home."

Epilogue

Life hadn't returned to normal. In fact, life might not ever be normal for Melinda again. As she nervously dressed to meet her brother, Jake Cochran, and his fiancée, attorney Cassidy Atkins, as well as her sister, architect Alexandra Golden, and her fiancé, ex-CIA agent Roarke Stone, for the very first time, she wondered for the hundredth time why Clay hadn't at least called her.

At first she'd made excuses for him. As head of his department he had to be extremely busy catching up and overseeing massive changes that had been a direct result of the congressional hearing. But after the first week had passed and she'd resumed her relationships with friends and gone back to work, she began to think that she really had imagined Clay's one-sentence declaration of love.

No one could be so busy that he couldn't spare sixty seconds for a phone call. By the second week, a feeling of constant anticipation settled in her stomach, which rolled into a tight knot every time her phone rang. Now, three weeks later, she no longer expected Clay to be on the other end of the phone when it rang. She'd lost hope and knew she had to go on with her life.

She'd worked full tilt on her plans to open the salon, bought new clothes for the big family get-together and gone through the motions of her life. But the future didn't seem as bright without Clay in it. During the day, she refused to think about the lonely tears she'd occasionally shed at night, but she couldn't stop the wonderfully erotic dreams that made her awaken wanting him so badly her heart ached.

She had to be sensible, relegate their experience to a fling and keep telling herself that someday it wouldn't hurt so much. She had to get a grip and put the past behind her.

She didn't feel ready to meet her siblings but could put it off no longer. An hour later, she drew a deep breath before entering the private hotel suite Jake had reserved for the family get-together. Pasting a smile on her face, Melinda knocked, determined to keep her private sorrows to herself.

When Clay opened the door with a wide smile, she thought she must be hallucinating. Her lower jaw dropped, leaving her mouth open. But she couldn't be imagining those broad shoulders, or his familiar green eyes or the mirth on lips scented with cherry gum. Still, she actually pinched her forearm to make sure she was awake.

"What are you—"

He cut off her question, sweeping her into his arms, his lips coming down hungrily on hers. Responding instinctively, she threw her arms around his neck, pressed herself against him. She heard vague cheering and clapping beyond the roar in her ears.

Her brother and sister! Oh God! What must they be thinking?

Mortified at her behavior, heat rushed to her face. She placed her palms on Clay's chest and pushed him back, embarrassment fueling her anger. "Just what the hell do you think you're doing, mister?"

"Little sister has a temper," she heard a male voice say with a masculine hum of amusement.

"I'm kissing you," Clay answered, his eyes looking as if he wanted to devour her whole.

"And doing a fine job of it, too," commented a dark-haired woman whose eyes were exactly the same whiskey shade as Melinda's and had to be her sister, Alexandra. Her sister was eyeing her with loving amusement and, despite her embarrassment, Melinda knew they would soon be the best of friends.

A tall man with dark hair, dark eyes and a serious demeanor except for the upward quirk of his lips tried to sound serious as he tapped Clay on the shoulder. "I'm assuming your intentions are honorable."

"Jake, stuff it." Cassidy, her brother's golden-haired fiancée, drew her arm through the crook of Jake's elbow and pulled him away after giving Melinda a friendly smile. "Let's see if you can kiss me like that."

Suddenly something beeped. Both her siblings and their future mates checked their beepers and phones. Clay leaned down and whispered in her ear. "I've missed you."

"You have a funny way of showing it. You couldn't find time to call?"

Jake looked suspiciously at her purse that continued to beep. "Maybe you should check your purse."

"I don't have a—"

Cassidy peered around Jake. "Something's definitely beeping in there."

Melinda opened her purse, intending to show them she didn't have a beeper, a pager or a cell phone. "You all aren't listening. I don't..." Her fingers closed around a soft velvet box that she didn't recognize. With a frown she plucked the beeping black velvet box from her purse.

"Open it," Clay told her, his eyes sparkling with mischief that told her he'd slipped the box into her purse during their embrace. She'd been so glad to see him, she hadn't noticed.

Still she hesitated.

Her sister nudged her. "Go on. Open it already."

Hands suddenly shaking, Melinda opened the box. And gasped. Inside was the most exquisite fiery opal surrounded by diamonds.

Clay touched the center stone and the beeping stopped. "Marry me?"

Her throat choked with tears. She wanted so badly to say yes, but she couldn't stand weeks and months and years of heartache like the last three. She didn't know if she could live with Clay putting his work first, always wondering when he would come home, feeling as if a phone call to him might interfere with a national emergency.

She snapped the box shut, pushed the ring into his hands. "You're already married."

"What?" Jake practically shouted.

"Calm down, Jake. Hot tempers seem to run in

your family, but I'm sure Clay's not a bigamist,'' Cassidy told her lover. "There must be another explanation.''

"Could we have a little privacy here?" Clay asked.

"Not a chance," Roarke, Alexandra's handsome friend, butted in as if he were family. From the way her sister looked adoringly at the man, Melinda expected the passion in their upcoming marriage to last through the years. "I think you owe us all an explanation.''

"He's married to his job," Melinda finally explained, sure her cheeks were showing her mortification.

Clay shook his head. "Not anymore.''

"You quit?" Jake arched a brow.

"I hired three assistants. And here's the best part.'' Clay grinned widely. "As head of the department, I've decided our old headquarters are insufficient. We're moving our operations center to a new location—in Daytona, Florida.''

Melinda glared at him through her tears. "Why didn't you tell me?''

"I just did.''

"Damn you, Clay.''

Jake nudged Alexandra. "With that temper, she's definitely our little sister.''

"Speak for yourself," Alexandra muttered. "I don't have a temper.''

Roarke whispered in her ear. "Guess I haven't riled you enough lately.''

Melinda ignored them and faced Clay with her hands fisted on her hips. "I don't hear from you for

three weeks, not one word, then you show up—"
tears flowed down Melinda's cheeks "—and you,
you…"

"I wanted all the details arranged before I sprang
the news. I wanted to surprise you. I wanted everything to be perfect so you wouldn't hesitate to be my
wife."

Melinda flung her arms around Clay's shoulders
and pulled his head down for a kiss.

Her family broke into whistles, claps and cheers.

Jake uncorked a bottle of champagne. "I think
Melinda just said *yes*."

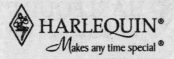

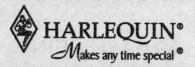

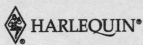
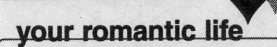

Coming in January 2002...

THE BEST MAN IN TEXAS
by
Kelsey Roberts

Lost:

One heiress. Sara Pierce wants to disappear permanently and so assumes another woman's identity. She hadn't counted on losing her memory....

Found:

One knight in shining armor. Dr. Justin Dale finds himself falling in love with his new patient...a woman who knows less about herself than he does.

Can the past be overcome, so that Sara and Justin may have a future together?

Finders Keepers: bringing families together

HARLEQUIN®
Makes any time special®

Visit us at www.eHarlequin.com

TBTCNM5

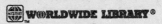

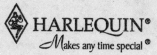